Jonathan Power

The Human Flow

An adventure story

Uncovering the Brutal Realities of West African Migrant Trafficking

Jonathan Power

THE HUMAN FLOW

AN ADVENTURE STORY

UNCOVERING THE BRUTAL REALITIES OF WEST AFRICAN MIGRANT TRAFFICKING

Bibliografische Information der Deutschen Nationalbibliothek
Die Deutsche Nationalbibliothek verzeichnet diese Publikation in der Deutschen Nationalbibliografie; detaillierte bibliografische Daten sind im Internet über http://dnb.d-nb.de abrufbar.

Bibliographic information published by the Deutsche Nationalbibliothek
Die Deutsche Nationalbibliothek lists this publication in the Deutsche Nationalbibliografie; detailed bibliographic data are available in the Internet at http://dnb.d-nb.de.

Cover art created with fotor.com

ISBN-13: 978-3-8382-1837-3
© *ibidem*-Verlag, Stuttgart 2023
Alle Rechte vorbehalten

Das Werk einschließlich aller seiner Teile ist urheberrechtlich geschützt. Jede Verwertung außerhalb der engen Grenzen des Urheberrechtsgesetzes ist ohne Zustimmung des Verlages unzulässig und strafbar. Dies gilt insbesondere für Vervielfältigungen, Übersetzungen, Mikroverfilmungen und elektronische Speicherformen sowie die Einspeicherung und Verarbeitung in elektronischen Systemen.

All rights reserved. No part of this publication may be reproduced, stored in or introduced into a retrieval system, or transmitted, in any form, or by any means (electronic, mechanical, photocopying, recording or otherwise) without the prior written permission of the publisher. Any person who does any unauthorized act in relation to this publication may be liable to criminal prosecution and civil claims for damages.

Printed in the EU

For my daughters, Carmen, Miri, Lucy and Jenny

July 5th 2023

I began my long, long, journey on a shaking bus. I was travelling from the up-country town of Iringa, once the regional capital of German-run Tanganyika, with its jacaranda trees smothered in blossoms of true purple—no better imperial legacy could there be—set haughtily amidst the dark, boulder-strewn, terrain of the Southern Highlands. The town had the smell of the early morning, silhouetted against the sky; the bus was fragrant with its added cargo of oranges. Everything uplifting and sharp, but the daytime heat would soon be upon us. Bit by jot the bus slowly edged itself down the mountainside to the Tanzanian capital, Dar-es-Salaam, residing on an extraordinary perfectly elliptical bay, facing the Indian Ocean, where the dhows flitted on their way to buy cloves in Zanzibar, and the sky appeared to be coloured with the hue of cobalt. Feather-light clouds cut thin lines from shore to horizon …

… I was tired. I was almost dizzy. I was dishevelled. I felt like a dead-beat, my legs dragged as though gravity had doubled itself. I felt unavailingly impotent. I was annoyed with my situation, their situation and the world's too. The poverty omnipresent all around me made me devoid of inspiration. I was squeezed out, my brain parched. My soul was exhausted. I withdrew and returned to the hotel. Deciding to take a swim in the hotel's lovely open-air pool I breast-stroked around, thinking all the time of my options.

Was she here in Nouakchott, the dried-up, desiccated, capital of Mauritania on the West African coast, was she there? There was no answer. I could only see ahead days of surmise and apprehension. A flirtation with catastrophe perhaps?

I asked directions to the bus terminal. It was a mass of bodies, pushing and shoving to get on the various buses. I asked one driver how I could find information on buses to Morocco. He pointed towards a man in the crowd wearing an official's hat. It was a struggle to make myself understood, but after persisting I got the idea that there was a bus tomorrow at six in the early morning as far as the border of Western Sahara, a state being fought over by Morocco and Algeria, whose battles rarely made the Western press. The Moroccans had the upper hand. Seemingly endless deposits of phosphate were the prize. The bus would take around 40 hours, including a night at the border.

At dinner, my batteries re-charged by couscous and Moroccan (Islamic, you can say) red wine, I decided to get a good night's sleep and then catch this early morning bus and make my hard and slow way to Morocco via Western Sahara. Maybe it would take three days since there was no through bus. If she didn't turn up at the iconic Casablanca hotel where we had always said we would rendezvous if things went wrong and we got separated, I could always come back to Nouakchott and start to toothcomb the city.

It was the thought—was it becoming love? —of Agnes which propelled me. I knew I'd do almost anything to find her, and it would take as long as it took.

I was up at five. The sun was slowly, ploddingly, over a placid, slate-like sea, making its way into the sky. It was refreshingly, stimulatingly cool, as I walked to the bus station. I'd bought another rucksack at one of the truck stops yesterday and I filled it up with water and food. I had no idea what the bus planned to do to keep us fed. I thought I would take no chances.

The bus was crowded. Not just with people and their babies but also with chickens, some strutting in the aisle. Somewhat to my surprise, I found the bus was air-conditioned. There was a toilet and a screen at the front that endlessly played Spanish, French and American war films. Is this the only thing they know about the West, I wondered? In my hotel there had been no BBC or CNN, nor Spanish and French programmes, much less anything that drew on Western culture. I presume these kinds of videos were their window on Europe and North America.

I had got myself a window seat and later was joined by a young man in his late twenties who said hello in French and proffered his hand. He gave me a broad smile. At 7ish the bus departed. We speeded too fast through the town, and I looked again at the shanty towns—if I didn't find Agnes in

Casablanca and had to retrace my steps where would I start?

All morning as we raced through the desert I could see the coast. The road stretched in what seemed an eternal emptiness in a phantom landscape, mysterious and eerie, where little, human or animal, moved, except the occasional cluster of camels and goats. By now the sun had climbed and the sea had turned into a mixture of blue and green, enticing. There was no wind and no waves. I started to enjoy it, only to be disillusioned when the tarmac ended, and the road became gravelly and bumpy. The bus was forced to slow, but not by much.

At noon we stopped in a village. Some of us walked around. A few including the driver dropped to their knees and said their prayers. I peed behind the back of the bus with the other men. Then it was the women's turn — the women always second in life all over Africa. Half an hour later we were on our way again. Back in the bus I pulled out my bread, a packet of imported liver pâté and some tomatoes.

I offered some to my neighbour who gave me a big smile and a thank you. We started to chat. He wasn't a migrant. He was going to Morocco to buy leather goods which he would bring back to Nouakchott to sell. He did this trip once a month, earning enough, he explained, to soon buy a decent house with a washing machine and television. He had three kids and his wife was pregnant again.

I told him my story. I gave him another sandwich. He looked a bit amazed as I narrated my tale, not least coming so far over the cruel and naked desert. "Well, it's possible she's in Casablanca," he said, "but don't be surprised if she isn't." "What do you mean?" I asked. "I don't want to alarm you, but there's a good chance she has been sold. A girl like that is worth a lot of money, as much as three or four Senegalese migrants, if not more."

"What would you do to track her down in Nouakchott?" I asked. "I would eliminate the shanty towns. She may have spent a couple of nights there, but she would have been sold very fast. Since she's educated, pretty, you say, and high class compared with the village girls here, she'd have ended up in some rich guy's house." "How would she be treated?" "Not well—not even pocket money. She would only be allowed out occasionally and then in the company of one of his wives and one of his guards—armed. She would be first for the bedroom and second to do the most menial chores is the house." "And if she refused the sex or tried to run away what would happen?" "He would beat her. Even if somehow, you tracked her down, you would never get to her. His house would be surrounded by high walls and there's bound to be a couple of armed guards on the gate. That's how the rich live here. If you tried to scale the wall they'd probably shoot you.

Slavery is so well ingrained in the culture here that even the government—which has tried—can't do much. The UN is

5

always on the government's back to abolish slavery, so are the EU and the African Union. The other countries in Africa think it gives Africa a bad name. But nothing happens." "Couldn't I go to the police?" "Ha, Ha! The police can be paid off. Forget it, forget her. My advice is go back home and find a new woman. Africa is full of beautiful women, black and beautiful, just like your Agnes."

Evening was coming and again the bus stopped in a small town on the sea. It was obvious that its people lived off fishing. There was a small café and shop and half the bus crowded in. In the end everyone seemed to get fed. When we got back to the bus there was a new driver. We drove through the night. It started to get cold. I was unprepared for this. I tossed and turned in my seat. It was absolutely a lousy night. The most uncomfortable and disagreeable I'd ever spent. There was a stillness all around, broken only by the sound of the wheels turning on the gravel, which seemed to make everything inside the sleeping bus even more silent and solitary. My new friend was out for the count, wrapped in a blanket. How I envied him. I drifted into the night, exhausted.

The dawn came as the sun, preparing as usual for its day of torturing us, rose out of the ocean. The highway along this stretch of remote, treacherous land seemed to go on forever. At 7 we stopped in another small fishing town. Again, we changed drivers. It was another day of driving. This time the road was tarred, and we could speed along a road that appeared to have no end in sight. Namibia made me feel small and insignificant. But after another two stops we were at the border of Western Sahara, the statelet that was 'occupied' by Morocco but fought over by Polisario which had long received help and refuge from neighbouring Algeria with its military government and Gaddafi's dictatorship in next door Libya. Indeed, post-Gaddafi Libya continues its support of Polisario.

Moroccan police manned the frontier. The driver asked us to disembark and show our passports. The police were polite to me but were curious about why I was making this long journey. I explained I was a journalist. I asked them about the traffickers. Did they come this way? "No," replied one of them, "They come off the road 10 kilometres or more back. They cut across the desert and pick up the road 10 kilometres into Western Sahara." Another interjected, "Occasionally we do capture one, but that's quite rare. We can't possibly police such a vast area of desert ... Anyway, our first concern is the Polisario fighters. We're overstretched."

We drove on northwards to Western Sahara's dilapidated capital, a small sand-filled town with a bunch of Moroccan flags lamely hanging dejectedly from poles around the town hall. My new friend told me that the bus terminated here, and I must change to a Moroccan bus. Then it would be another half-day's drive. He advised me to do what he intended to do: spend the night in a little hotel he knew and get some sleep and decent food. There were three or four buses a day up to the Moroccan border proper. There in the morning we could catch a bus to Casablanca. He was going there too. He knew the city quite well. He would direct me to my hotel.

The next evening our bus rolled into Casablanca. He put me in a taxi and told the driver where to take me. "I'm staying in the Hotel Sahara. Remember that. I'm here for a week and if you need help come and find me. Better still, phone me." He gave me his number. Ten minutes later I was in the forecourt of the Casablanca hotel, paying the taxi what seemed like a pittance, but that's all the driver asked for. In the lobby there were big photos of Humphrey Bogart, Ingrid Bergman and the hotel's piano player, Dooley Wilson, who played Sam and sang "As Time Goes By," an immortal piece of music. Tattooed on the wall behind the piano was the everlasting line by Lisa (Bergman): "Play it again, Sam."

***

Some weeks earlier

Let me stop there. This story actually begins in Tanzania. I'd been living in a village and working advising peasant farmers on how to increase their lowly incomes. Idealistic my friends said. In fact, I hadn't many options since I only had a third class degree in tropical agricultural economics.

I had taken the bus from where I lived in the Southern Highlands to the capital, Dar-es-Salaam, where I wanted to talk to the editor of the local newspaper to see if I could persuade him to let me write some articles about living up-country where, apart from the locals, only a few haggard leftovers from the British colonial service were still residing. The editor, a tall white-haired man, himself a better kind of leftover — one of the few idealists, I suspected — seemed favourable to me writing. After a coffee he walked me round the newsroom, briefly chatting to those we passed in the corridor, with his cheerful bonhomie highlighting his obvious lack of racism, which was still prevalent among the residual white population, and introduced me to a young African woman, Agnes, around my age, who ran the opinion desk. We talked about where I'd come from and what exactly her job was. The editor left me to it. She invited me to pull up a chair. I liked her from the start—bright and thoughtful. I thought, why not ask her out for a drink? We were about the same age—mid to late twenties. We made a date to go for a swim in the warm sea—her suggestion—when she finished work and after to talk over a beer in a beach café. In the sea I couldn't help but notice her lithe, lissom, figure, but also her high forehead and her intelligent looks. She had an amusing way of crinkling her pretty face when she laughed. Her swimsuit was finely cut and, to say the least, a little provocative. Despite being old enough to have finished a masters at university a year before, she looked like a precocious teenager, fresh out of childhood. After chatting a while, I could see why the editor had put her in charge at the opinion desk. She could talk about everything from politics to the worth of foreign aid to literature. Her Oxford education showed. Very few black students were admitted to Oxford in our day—there was a built-in discriminatory system that favoured those from public and top grammar schools and highly educated, well-placed, families. (Mind you, it's still true, albeit improving fast.) She fascinated me from the word go. The celibate me could barely control myself. I'd only had two girlfriends. And they were on kissing terms, full stop.

A while later, having manoeuvred around a Portuguese-man-of war jelly fish with its long tentacles and an excruciatingly painful sting—a danger here much more common than sharks—and then drunk a couple of locally brewed beers, I took her hand and leaned over the table and kissed her. To my utter surprise she didn't pull away. Instead, she took hold of my hand and stroked it.

To take my mind off my feelings I talked about my hopes for Africa, about how my urge to do right by a continent few in Europe or America gave much attention to unless there was a famine, coup d'état or a war—all of which happened much less than they used to. I started on my favourite subject: "Public opinion is led by the nose by the media who think, 'If it bleeds it leads'. We aren't very aware of new trends in Africa— big improvements in agriculture and a sharply increased rate of long-term economic growth, high-tech start-ups, the very rapid spread of mobile phones, a big sale of smart phones, a sizeable film industry in Nigeria, fashion houses with amazing designers and innovative ways of using phones—like giving medical advice over the phone. In some areas in the phone business, it's ahead of Europe." I was starting to get steamed up. "I know lots of people criticise foreign aid but when well used it has primed many a pump, leading to increased government social spending which has resulted in steady falls in infant mortality, the rapid slowing of deaths of women in childbirth and the provision of clean water. Smallpox, Polio and River Blindness have been eradicated from every village and town in the continent, there's a new vaccine for Ebola and a lot of progress has been made on eliminating Malaria, a scourge that lays low half of Africa at one time or another. A new vaccine seems to be effective. Rates of Covid infection have been low. The European idea of the dark continent just irritates me. What's dark is our ignorance of it."

Her eyes were all attentive. She gave me a high-five. "Not a bad speech for an imperialist," she said, grinning. She told me she had studied politics and economics at Oxford, how she had worked for a year on the Oxford Times and had eyed Fleet Street in London for a job on a national paper. But then her father summoned her back home as her mother had been found riddled with cancer, and here she was on a smallish paper, wondering what to do next and how to do it.

I told her about my time in Lesotho, doing an internship during my third year, and my thesis on migration and the debilitating effect it had on both the migrant males and their families left at home to farm a small plot and to wait anxiously for the monthly remittance payments.

What was the point of Africans fighting for independence in Lesotho and South Africa if the lifeblood was being drained out of their peasantry by the demands of the gold, platinum, lithium, cobalt and diamond mines, desperate for cheap labour?

We ate, we drank, we occasionally kissed quick ones and in the end agreed we would try and get a major British paper to sponsor an in-depth investigation of this. But we had no contacts.

She asked her editor in chief if he had a contact in London. He didn't but he did have on a Johannesburg paper. We wrote a letter with a summary of our idea. Two weeks later we had a reply. The editor liked it but wrote, "We are up to our eyes in the Southern African migrant story. Why don't you look at it in another part of Africa? Our readers would like to know about the travails of immigration in West Africa." He knew more than we did — about Senegal, Mali, Mauritania and Nigeria. They were off the map for both me and Agnes.

I'd had to get the bus back to Iringa the next day. I said farewell to Agnes, kissing behind the bus. "Bye Jon," she said, looking rather doleful. As we stood by the entrance to the bus she said she would wait for the reply of the South African editor to our proposal and how much he would pay us upfront. She would immediately let me know what he said. "As soon as the letter arrives, I'll write to you. I'm sure it will be a 'yes'."

It was a 'yes'. Within two days of her getting his reply I received her letter brimming with excitement. She had written back to him, asking for a fee and guaranteed expenses for the two of us. Her credentials looked good to a white South African liberal. She "sold" me as the necessary partner as I spoke French.

Two weeks later I set off for Dar-es-Salaam. Agnes was waiting for me and took me straight to the white beach to swim, with transparent blue-green water and tall palm trees lining the shore, waving like ballerinas in the tropical breeze. After dinner she dropped me off at the youth hostel. The next day we were airborne on Ethiopian Airlines, the continent's best, founded in the 1950s with no crash in its record until a new Boeing hurtled into the ground at the beginning of 2019, as a result of faulty technology installed by its maker. It had been started by the American airline, TWA, but its pilots and ground staff had long departed. This was a true African airline with all black crews. Sometimes, a newspaper report said, they had all female Ethiopian crews. It was the only one that crossed the continent, hence our long way round. The next day, early in the morning, the first, sharp, almost white, light reflecting off the plane's long wings, we landed in Dakar, the capital of Senegal.

What is there ever to do on a plane? For me it's writing. I'd decided to write an article for the Dar-es-Salaam paper about the airline. I chatted with the cabin staff to glean some more background. For Agnes it was reading a novel and interrupting me. I loved it. Her eyes gleamed as she told me about her life in Oxford. "I'll never forget Oxford. I learnt things I never knew existed. I read hundreds of novels and poetry books — from Chaucer to Graham Greene. I had teachers like Isaiah Berlin and A.J.P. Taylor. I met a boy I liked, Welsh, and lost my virginity."

We drank lots of wine, kissed a lot and got rather tipsy. It was a five-hour flight across the continent. I began to feel intoxicated in more ways than one. I felt I was becoming incandescent, feverish, craving her. So sexually charged I was, I wasn't presentable enough to stand up in front of all those passengers, but I desperately needed to go to the loo. Agnes and I hadn't discussed sex, but I had to tell her my condition. "I tell you what," she said giggling. "I'll come with you. Stand close behind me and follow me down the aisle. Nobody will notice!"

It broke the ice. My mind was in a rotating twirl, ready to spew out my momentary thoughts — and lusts. A drink later I told her I wanted to make love to her. She laughed. "I bet you do. You must be the hundredth man who has told me that. I'm picky." She put her head in her book and I realised the conversation was over for now. I started to re-read Alan Paton's novel, "Cry, The Beloved Country." No other novel had so affected me during my research in the mountains of Lesotho when in the evenings in my tent all I had for company was this book. It took me right into the storm centre of South Africa's apartheid and the naked evil of migration to the mines. The trauma of migration took on a new life. Every word rang with excruciating pain. How can men so exploit their fellow humans? These days on Sundays the whites no longer go to church, they go to Ikea. Morality has become an empty vessel. Of course, I told myself, it's always been a bit like this. Lip service wasn't introduced in 1963, the year when amoral consumerism took over Britain and among the whites in Britain's imperial empire, as the poet Philip Larkin might have written. (Recall his poem: "Sexual intercourse began/ in nineteen sixty-three/ which was rather late for me/ Between the end of the "Chatterley" ban/ And the Beatles first LP.")

By now I've read numerous novels written by non-South African blacks, like Ngũgĩ wa Thiong'o from Kenya and Chinua Achebe from Nigeria. Nigeria has become a veritable literary factory producing especially good novels. Wole Soyinka won the Nobel Prize for literature and Ben Okri won the world's top prize for writers in English, the Booker, with "The Famished Road." And just two years ago, Abdulrazak Gurnah from Zanzibar won the Nobel Prize. Nigerian women too have joined the industry to great international acclaim, like Chimamanda Ngozi Adiche, Helen Oyeyemi, Ayobami Adebayo and Chigozie Obioma. The latter was on the long list to win the Booker prize. Another Nigerian novelist, Bernadine Evaristo, won it the year before last. (Note the Brazilian surname. Many Brazilian blacks once slavery was abolished returned home to where their forefathers lived.) But none of these novelists opened my eyes to the horror of migration as Paton's did.

"My favourite African novel," I leaned over and told Agnes, is "The Famished Road." I wanted to show I wasn't put out by her hurting remark. "The writing is so powerful. I don't know how Ben Okri does it. He throws words up in the air and like diamonds, rubies, emeralds and silver they catch the sun and dazzle before they fall and hit the page." "I wish you could read it to me," Agnes said and made to go back to her book. "Agnes, I've got a copy in my rucksack. I want to re-read it when we arrive in West Africa. It will help me get the atmosphere. And I *will* read it to you." I had no idea that Senegal was totally different from Nigeria.

I retrieved my copy and read to her a part I'd marked: "The old woman in the forest pressed on with the weaving of our true secret history. A history that was frightening and wondrous, bloody and comic, labyrinthine, circular, always turning, always surprising, with events becoming signs and signs becoming reality. The old woman in the forest coded the secrets of plants and their infinite curative properties; she coded the language of spirits, the epic speech of trees, the convergent lines of vital earth-forces, the healing uses of thunder, the magic properties of lightening, the interpretations of the human and spiritual world, the delicate balances of unseen powers and the ancient formula for glimpsing the unalterable movement of fate. She even coded fragments of the great jigsaw that the creator spread all over the diverse peoples of the earth, hinting that no one race or people can have the complete picture or monopoly of the ultimate possibilities of the human genius alone. With her magic she suggested that it's only when all peoples meet and know and love one another that we begin to get an inkling of the awesome picture or jigsaw of majestic power."

"Wow, that is amazing literature!" Agnes said. "I feel bad I'm so ignorant of the writing of my own continent. That's what comes of studying at Oxford. Dead white males are all we read."

"Will you read a few pages to me every evening on this trip? I like your voice too. So crystal clear, like an actor or BBC presenter!" "Sure," I said. "Why not? I'd enjoy it too — round a campfire would be good — in the forest." "I don't think there's much forest where we are going," Agnes said, laughing. Her white teeth made that smile of hers come to life. "Well, I'd better stop myself there. Any more kissing and I'll be a goner."

We got off the plane in Dakar. This is a tourist country so they make it easy to get through passport control and customs. Within 15 minutes we were on our way in a new-looking taxi to a little hotel, someone on the plane had told me about as I waited self-consciously in the queue for the bathroom. By chatting I hoped I'd distract him from my condition. The hotel was run by a bustling late middle-aged French woman. The hotel was a melange of French and African styles. We both liked it. "Let's drop our bags off in our rooms and meet down here for a drink," I suggested, "and then we can think about dinner and where to go."

After a cold orange juice we got a taxi to a place Madame recommended on the beach. "It's quite small, too simple for most tourists," she said, "but the fish is today's catch. You can get beer but not wine, but I've got plenty of French wine and brandy when you get back. My husband and I used to go there. He loved it but he died last year, and I don't want to go alone and trigger my memories."

There was good local fish, cooked over a charcoal fire with fried chicken, cashew nuts, rice and plantains, and iced beer and waves running up the beach as the leisurely tide came in. Stars, as bright, illuminated and luminous as in Tanzania, but this was a different sky since we had crossed the equator and now were in the northern hemisphere. The sky had been paved with the darkness of the night. I wanted to embrace it and hold too the vastness of the sea. If something as beautiful as the sea and sky exist, then life must be beautiful too. I had thought that for many years, as I was a city boy. A journey to look at the sea was always a peak experience that brought peace to my regular bouts of melancholia.

We decided to walk back to the hotel. Holding Agnes's hand seemed natural. We could see the paraffin lights in the village. There was the occasional passing person on the empty track. We always stopped for two or three minutes to say hello and for them to ask where we were going. I think both of us felt very safe.

Eventually we hit the main road just as an old, rattling, bus came round the corner. We flagged it down and ended up half an hour later in Dakar's bus station, five minutes' walk from the hotel.

Madame Chevalier was still up, serving a group of Senegalese. A glass of wine and three big brandies later we stumbled upstairs. We kissed in a rather drunken way and could hardly stop, but still I managed to hold back. Besides, there was no indication from Agnes that she was prepared to go further. I got the feeling if I made a move she would laugh at me again, just as she had on the plane.

***

The piercing African light woke us both up early. The sun burned in the sky like a fever dream. As I looked out of the wide window it appeared as if everything was becoming primary and elementary: the colours, the shapes and perimeters of the buildings. Already I could feel the heat, wrenching, probably later lacerating, interlaced by the smell of the tropical sea which has an odour of its own that comes from the many kinds of seaweed in southern latitudes. I smiled at Agnes as she descended the stairs, ever so refined and confident. I wondered how I seemed to her.

After a very French breakfast we headed off to one of the big, overflowing, shanty towns—what the French and Senegalese call a bidonville—that we had noticed on the road coming in from the airport. Bidonvilles exist all over Africa. They are settlements, built almost in a day and a night, a week at the most, housing new arrivals from the countryside, people desperate to find jobs. They contain their own tribal neighbourhoods, speaking their own languages and practising their own customs. They centre their settlements around a well. Apart from water the dwellings have hardly any urban necessities—no sewerage, rarely electricity and only a few schools or health clinics. The rubbish putrefies in the gutter. For decades they were seen as a temporary phenomenon, so the government more or less ignored them. As the years rolled by and they expanded their tentacles fast the government was compelled to think about the long-term. In Senegal, which is a fairly well-run, long-time, democracy, they decided to upgrade the settlements in situ, rather than build new houses. Water, electricity and sewerage were brought in. Primary schools and clinics were constructed. But these only attracted more peasants from the countryside. It has become a race between the local authorities and their creation of public utilities and the rate of arrival of new proletarians. As in Europe and North America immigrants can overwhelm the locals and those who settled before them. The creation of jobs cannot keep up. Some push off northwards to Europe—the lonely Dick Whittingtons of the desert.

We had no idea on how to start finding someone who would know about migration to Europe. We asked if there was a school in the first neighbourhood we arrived at. There was. We managed to find the headmaster. He was surprised to be confronted by two journalists, one white and one black, but not as surprised as if we had turned up in its east African ex-British counterpart. The French, unlike those of Anglo and Dutch stock, have always accepted mixed couples. Indeed, the late president, Leopold Senghor, had been a member of the French cabinet, married a white woman and his volumes of Negritude poems were good sellers among the cognoscenti in France.

We told him who we were looking for — someone who knew about the trafficking to Paris. He knew about it, telling us he despaired of its effect. He knew so many children bereft of a father. They did badly in school and provided more than their fair share of the unruly. He gave us the address of the local government administrator who might know more.

We saw him and got another lead and then another and then another, as we were constantly recommended to someone else. Nobody seemed to know or, if they did, pretended they knew nothing. This indeed was clandestine traffic. We sweated it out for four days and must have tramped miles around the tin and cardboard shacks of the newcomers and the more solid mud houses of the established residents.

The city government had done quite a good job in this shanty town. There were water stands and electricity. Buses connected people with the rest of the city. Most people, we were told, could find jobs of some kind — the lowest tiers of work — in shops, driving vans and taxis or in the peanut factories. Peanuts are Senegal's main cash crop. Still, as we had been told by the headmaster, a quarter of the population was unemployed. Crime was ubiquitous.

As we walked around, I began to feel I could write a thesis on this place and how it worked. I seemed to learn about everything, except what we wanted to know. Agnes was getting very fed up. I could see it in her eyes that were often half closed. We were both becoming demoralised and disillusioned. It showed. However drunk we got in the evening there was less kissing. Romance no longer frittered inside either of us. I began to feel we were on the road to nowhere.

Totally unexpectedly on the fifth day we got a lead. I'd told Agnes that she must do the talking as I think when I talked I maybe frightened people off. White men were a rarity hereabouts and one asking questions an object of suspicion. I sat myself in a tatty looking teashop and Agnes strolled off to the address she'd been given. Her schoolgirl French wasn't so good, but like many Africans she had an ear for languages. In four days of almost continuous conversation it had improved remarkably.

An hour later I saw her coming down the hill with its sprawling houses and cavorting children to the teashop. Small kids rolling hoops ran beside her, laughing, shouting, sometimes falling over as they sped down the hill too fast. She was smiling. "You must come with me. I've found an oldish fella who is prepared to talk. He says that for ten years he was a trafficker. But now he had made some money he was retired, living with his son's family." We could see two shiny new Peugeots parked outside his house. The house itself was quite large with a new roof. There was even a sizeable garden. Inside, as I found later, the toilet had a modern chemical disposal system. The bathroom was tiled, and the sink and bath had ostentatious imitation gold taps. The kitchen was prim and shiny, a new oven and washing machine in place.

He certainly knew his business. He knew the routes across the Sahara. He knew where we would find Senegalese traffickers. He knew how to hire a boat across to Gibraltar and he knew how to find a Spanish lorry driver there who would take 20 migrants at a time, crammed in the back, up to Paris. There he used to hand his load of men over to the big boss who ran one of the abandoned factories where the men stayed.

He talked on, rather liking our earnest questions and countenance, I suspected. After two hours of talk we ended up with five pages of my notebook full of names, directions and even a crude map of the way the migrants took. We had begun with locally grown tea and we were now on to imported beer. "You must take the train, the one that goes right up to Ouagadougou in Mali. It goes every other evening and it will take you nearly 10 hours. You must get off at Bakel. You will be on the Senegal side of the border of Mauritania. The river divides the countries. Get a lift into the town. I'm going to give you the name of my contact there, and a letter to the local chief." I handed him €50. He gave a slight bow, smiling.

That evening we caught the old train that looked as if it was on its last legs. It was completely dilapidated, rust-ridden and obviously never cleaned on the dirt-coloured outside. It chugged along at no more than 80 kilometres an hour. To our surprise we had clean sheets in our first-class bunk beds, one on top of the other, a restaurant with good straightforward food — a steak and French fries, and even wine. Some things the French colonialists had done well, not just building a railway but introducing a train culture that made sure good wine and steak were always available.

It got dark. The carriage lights were dim. We couldn't read any more. We decided to go to bed. Agnes took the top bunk. I felt a bit peculiar. Here I was on a train in what was still for me, even after a year of living in Tanzania, a strange and unknown continent, lying close by one of its own, moving into its dark interior following the steps of the great explorers, much faster than they could ever have imagined as, on foot, they hacked themselves through the long, sharp-ended, savannah grass. And who was I? A neo-colonialist? Certainly not. But I was an exploiter in a different form, earning a living, far better than the peasants asleep in the villages beside the rail line, off their experiences. My thoughts drifted. What kind of human being did I aspire to be? Strip off the need to have a job or a partner, what was underneath? I realized I was full of paradoxes. I was very get up and go, but also I hated being alone without a woman for company, even if it was just a platonic friendship. I was too often hypocritical. I could fudge my core beliefs, sometimes too easily. I believed in helping the poor and, as I did in Tanzania, living close to them as I did in a village but I certainly wasn't going to accept their level of health care. When needed I would go to the paying hospital that 90% of the Africans couldn't afford. And what did I do about the beggars in the street? Nothing, apart from the odd few coins. Confrontation with beggars or very poor people often left me confused about myself. They had their life, I often thought, and it was on a different planet to mine. I couldn't push myself to where I thought in my mind I should go—to give all of myself to those who, if I couldn't help in a total sense, I could help more than I was doing now. I'd met priests and nuns in Tanzania who lived right in the city's slums. I was far away from them. I didn't like myself for that. I wanted some fun in my life and some money for holidays on a beach or to take a woman to the expensive opera or ballet when I visited London.

I don't know how long I'd been asleep but I woke feeling enormously roused. I couldn't stop thinking about making love to Agnes. I tried to get back to sleep but a great sexual urge kept sweeping over me in waves. I got out of bed, touched Agnes's hand and stroked it. She half opened her eyes. "Can I come up into your bed?" I asked. She nodded. I climbed up her ladder and in a moment our bodies were entwined. I felt myself being swept away by an incontrollable mass of feelings. We began to kiss. I cupped her breast. Before what seemed like a moment had passed I was inside her. My intelligence and my emotions parted company. She stroked my back. I felt myself about to ejaculate. I started to sob and to shout. Her body began to shake. She kissed me wildly. My first sex, and we had, within three minutes, climaxed at the same time. I was filled with an ecstasy such as I'd never known. I lay still, overcome. Agnes had drained me of willpower. I had the sensation I was being gored in the centre of my heart. I could hear the rumbling of the train. There was a dull light up in the ceiling. I could see that her body was slenderer and more docile than when she had had her clothes on. Once was enough, more than enough. Before I fell asleep I wondered for a few seconds when I would feel self-assured enough about my sexual power and potency. I'd heard all sorts of things about how to satisfy a woman, and I was aware on this first occasion I had a way to go. Yet for me at that moment it was total fulfilment and happiness beyond all measure. We fell asleep with our arms wrapped around each other.

We woke with first light—a soft but burning sun touching the few fluffy clouds. Immediately, I sat up and looked at Agnes beside me. What was this all about, I asked myself—just a summer lightning of passion and mutual discovery or something richer and deeper? We could smell coffee and we padded along to the restaurant car. The cook produced some fresh-baked croissants and jam, but no butter, and we chewed contentedly as the train wound through the scrub land—not quite desert but a parched, scorched and arid landscape. Alongside the thorn bushes were small plots of hoed land. I assumed they were growing peanuts, one of Senegal's staple foods, easily grown in arid soils, and an important export. We crossed a trickle of a stream. Lined along its bank were donkeys drinking and behind them, parked, were carts. The train trundled along. We could see these donkey carts everywhere we looked. Sometimes just a driver with a load of bags of charcoal or thatching material. Sometimes with his wife heading for the nearest town which the train's waiter had told us was about 10 minutes ahead.

The train stopped but there was no station and no town. We were told to get off. There were dozens of these donkey carts. Agnes hailed one and told me to hop on. I felt a little panic-stricken as the train slowly pulled away and I knew there wasn't another for two days. We were on our own, our retreat cut off. One side of me was anxious, nervous. The other was curious and inquisitive. Where and with what did these women acquire their gorgeous dresses? They looked like they'd been dressed for a Parisian wedding with great lengths of brilliant cotton cut to sophisticated perfection and carefully turned bright turbans to match. What style they had, looking so confident and poised as if they were riding on air, and yet I knew they were downright poor. I wouldn't find out until tomorrow the answer to this paradox.

It was a good half hour bumpy ride into Bakel. It was an old-fashioned clip clop ride along a sandy trail. We were part of a long line of passengers from the train, many loaded with suitcases and boxes. Most of the donkeys were overloaded, overworked and tired and we passed them one after the other. I always looked as we overtook to see if we were being studied. It can't be every day, I thought, that a black and white couple were seen out here. Yet we appeared to be part of the landscape and then I reminded myself that the president was married to a white French woman.

We arrived at the small dusty town. It looked as if it hadn't changed in a hundred years. It sank into the desert scrub. There were spikes of aloe along the side of the rutted streets. There was an occasional motorised taxi and plenty more donkey carts. The main streets were planted with desiccated trees which offered some shade from the sun that drummed into every inhabitant, human or animal. People moved around at a crawl. Somnolence is too mild a word to describe the lethargy that infused the town like stale tea leaves. "So this is the home to groups of traffickers who cross the desert with migrants," I said to Agnes. "Sure is," she replied. "Now we have to find them, but let's first wander around, get a snack and a big drink of water and then go and see the local consul." "That sounds like a good program to me."

We walked around and found a lean-to café with a roof made of palm tree leaves. "Oh God," I said. "Thank you for the shade." The sun had demolished me in the hour since we had got off the train. There were a few men in the cafe but no women. We learnt later that the men hardly work when they're home. Their old occupations of war and cattle rearing had disappeared for different reasons. The first because of French colonialism which stamped out the inter-tribal fighting which employed the men, as it carved out a state. Senegal was a province of the great French West African Empire that was transformed into a half a dozen states as the empire broke up in the 1960s when independence became the rallying cry. The second was the fault of the encroaching Sahara. Over-cultivation and the early signs of climate change had undermined animal food supply. This was why migration had become almost the only possibility. These men, we soon found out, after buying them a beer, were recently back home from France after two years away.

Re-hydrated, we asked the way to the consul's office. Every region in Senegal has a consul, responsible for administering often a vast area. Built on a bluff, on the edge of the town, the consulate was an imposing building. The consul was welcoming but rather aloof, well aware he was the only educated man within a hundred kilometres. Nevertheless, he was clearly glad to see us and be able to have a conversation at a level he couldn't have with the locals. I wondered how he could survive this isolation even though he had a wife and family. He introduced us to his wife, a demure woman, who beneath her flowered dress walked in high heels and clearly, if quietly, I thought, carried herself as if she believed she was the most elegant woman in town — which she probably was. Soon she left the room to get us some tea. The way the French had built the administrative structure meant that aspiring bureaucrats of talent had to spend five years in the remoter regions. The Senegalese had continued this practice after independence.

In an hour we learnt from him more about the migrant traffic than we had learnt in a week in Dakar.

"Time for lunch," said Agnes, as we walked back into town feeling good. "We have arrived at the right place. Now we need to meet some more of the locals. We have the name of the village chief and an introduction to a trafficker. After we've eaten let's go and pay them a visit."

Lunch was in a little, nondescript, hidden-away, café we wouldn't have found if the consul hadn't told us where we could eat. There was only one thing on the menu — a goat meat stew. Goats which can live on scrub and who were herded by small boys were the only source of meat around, apart from pigs and chickens.

"I'm already tired," I moaned to Agnes. "How hot do you think it is?" "It's going to get worse when we get right out into the desert," she laughed. "But don't think because I have a black skin I don't feel this heat. Don't you know Africans too can get sun stroke or develop skin cancer?"

We started our interviews in the café — in French which locals could speak, if not well. I had difficulty in understanding them but Agnes seemed to get the gist. What we wanted to know is where did the traffickers operate from — home, a street corner or perhaps even an office. Did they know, we asked the waitress, the cook and then the owner, how to find some of them?

"If you sit right here long enough," observed the owner, "one of them will come in here to have a beer or a bite to eat."

We agreed waiting was a good idea. Indeed, an hour later a well-dressed man came in for a beer. By "well-dressed" I don't mean a suit and tie, but a flowing robe of blue and yellow with white brocade, carefully hand sewn, around the edges. Agnes went over and introduced us and explained what we wanted to know. I wanted to say, "off the record." But since our French didn't have that word and since out here up country, in the outback, they wouldn't know the expression, I said nothing. Quickly, Agnes told him with her dazzling smile that it was all for a book that probably wouldn't be published for two years, and all names would be made anonymous.

I bought the three of us a beer and we sat down to talk. It was a convivial conversation. He was amazed we had come all the way from Tanzania. He told us he had got into the trafficking business because his village had suffered from a long drought, and this was the only work he could find. He'd inherited a lorry from his well-to-do father who had been a peanut trader. He preferred this job rather than being a migrant himself because he didn't want to go so far away from home. Besides his family, a wife and children whom he loved, his old mother was sickly, and he needed to be close by for her.

He didn't mention that traffickers had a reputation for being greedy about money, earned a lot and weren't afraid of dumping one of their charges in the desert if they didn't cough up some more money. Often by the time a migrant reached Paris or wherever they were heading they were stone-broke, their savings to help them get started gone. There at their destination they would have to borrow money from a loan shark, running up a debt that eradicated a quarter of the minimal wages they earned. Sure, it was better to be a trafficker if you had some money and a truck or an organisation behind you.

We egged him on and a few beers later he became quite loquacious and offered to introduce us to some of the other traffickers in town. We showed him the letter of introduction we had and he said that was addressed to his brother. Our ball was rolling.

Beer was the bribe of choice. The bigger the bribe, the more his friends talked. They weren't bothered about talking to journalists. Apart from the lone consul, few bureaucrats or journalists ventured this far from their air-conditioned offices in Dakar.

They told us the best route across the Sahara was to drive up to the Mauritanian border and strike north west from there, aiming first for Nouakchott, the capital, and then for Morocco.

It took about two to three days to Nouakchott, and they only carried enough water for that—water was heavy and more meant less room for more migrants. At the northern Mauritanian border they handed over their cargo to Moroccan traffickers who packed the migrants into their lorries and drove up by way of Morocco to Tangiers for the short sail to Spain. Here they handed their cargoes over to Spanish traffickers. They drove the immigrants up to Paris, Lyons, Marseilles, Tours or Lille. (I later learnt there were alternative routes across the Mediterranean from Libya and Tunis.)

"What do you charge?" asked Agnes. They looked at each other and said nothing. Agnes gave each of them her gorgeous smile. "I swear on my mother's grave I won't tell anybody. Just give me an idea." The youngest of the men—I guess about 25—spoke. "Around €500 each to the coast. On top of that another €100 each if we have to bribe the police. Then the Moroccan and Spanish guys need to be paid. I think about another €1000 for them." "How on earth does a villager find that kind of money?" One of the older men joined the discussion. "Twenty years ago you could do the whole journey for a third of that. These men go to work in Dakar for a while and save their earnings. They borrow from their relatives in Dakar and in the village back home." "Aren't they frightened they would never recover their loans?" interjected Agnes. "All this could only happen because these men promise to send back money to pay the debt and then a new young relative can do the same journey. It goes on like this. The members of a man's village would never let him default. That would make the village an outlaw that traffickers wouldn't want to be bothered with." So that's how the pump was primed, I thought to myself.

"And how much do you make? How many migrants a month do you take across the desert?" About €10,000 a month, to be shared among five of us," the older man said. "There are four trucks in a convoy. We are taking around 80 on each trip—20 men in each lorry."

I looked at the new-looking Toyotas parked outside the bar.

"Isn't it very dangerous?" I asked. They nodded. One of the younger men said he'd heard the other day of one of the trucks slipping, overturning and then tumbling down a sand dune. Six died. There were about 25 men in the truck. It was overloaded. Another of the men said, "I heard recently of some driver finding the bodies of 15 migrants including 5 teenage children. There are some guys who ask their truckload for more money and if they don't pay up they abandon them in the desert." "We never do that." He screwed up his face in distaste.

"It's very difficult to find your way. Sometimes the wind blows the sand over the tracks. But we have GPS now, so that makes it a lot easier. But not that long ago we got lost before I'd bought my GPS machine. I guess I was lucky. It's never happened to me since."

We asked if we could meet them tomorrow. 10 in the morning, I suggested. They nodded. We wandered off to have a look around the sand-drenched town for the first time. It was the usual African higgly-piggly agglomeration — huts, chickens, goats and women pounding cassava — a good root staple that grows anywhere and contains both carbohydrates and vitamins. In Dakar they regard it as village food and people switch to expensive imported, less nutritious, white rice as soon as they have the means. There would be less hunger and malnutrition in Africa if local governments encouraged people to eat indigenous nutritious crops like cassava, yams and bananas. The chickens, like the small, skipping, children and mangy dogs, were everywhere. We couldn't work out how each owner knew which was their hen or cock.

The huts were much bigger than the ones I knew in Tanzania. Some were built of brick, not mud and wood. Some had little gardens out front, and I could see the occasional, rather dried up, wilting tomato plant.

Around one corner we came upon a quite unusual site, at least not one I'd seen anywhere I had travelled before. Sitting on a stool in the open air, there was a woman with a weaving loom in front of her. Coming out of the loom on the other side was a good two metres of cloth in a gorgeous blue. The whole scene looked like an alpine horn giving birth. Now I knew where my smuggler had bought his cloth. By the odd look of the loom it clearly was not made in Manchester. I guess some ironsmith in the town had built it.

We were thirsty. We found a very simple bar, but it had a fridge and we ordered a Coke. It is a fact that Coke and Pepsi can be found all over Africa, but water can sometimes be hard to find. The reason why is that the soft drinks are distributed by private companies. The other things that people want — water, seeds and fertilizer are often distributed or organised by bureaucratic, slow-moving government agencies.

"Where are we going to sleep tonight?" I asked Agnes. "I guess you didn't hear what the consul said," she laughed. "He suggested we go and ask that question to the town's chief. Also, remember in Dakar the ex-trafficker gave us a letter of introduction."

The owner of the bar gave us directions. The house was quite a bit bigger than the others. We knocked on the door. We were lucky. The chief was at home and invited us in for tea. One of his wives made the tea but shy, I guessed, didn't join us, although Agnes had waved 'come over'.

We told him about the book we were writing. He was interested and started to chat about how he wished these young men would stay at home and till the land. "It's not good for family life if they go far away."

"On the other hand we have a new mosque that the migrants helped us pay for. And migrants from the same village often club together to buy things like a hand pump for the well. That's better than a bucket on a rope."

We chatted on. Of course, he wanted to know what we did in Tanzania and why we had journeyed all the way from Dar-es-Salaam to here. We asked him if there was a little hotel in town. "You must stay with me," he said. "Oh, you are very kind," said Agnes. "We'll dump our bags if we may. We want to wander around a bit more and see if we can find some young men to talk to. We'll be back before sunset."

"I'm so hot and tired," I said, as we walked away. "This sun knocks the life out of me. Tanzania is cool compared with here. Look, there's something that looks like a children's swing and a shade tree. Maybe there's room for us to lie down next to it." We slept for a good hour and then woke up to find a ring of children round us who probably had never seen a white man before. "Since you were lying down" teased Agnes, "they may have thought you'd dropped out of the sky!"

"I don't feel like doing any more talking today. I just want to lie down on a cool bed and make love to you. I've only done it once in my life as you know and I'm hungry for more." "Well, you will just have to tie a knot in it." She skipped away before I could smack her. "Tonight," I said, "if the chief is kissing one wife after another and the women are moaning, I won't be able to contain myself."

We found another restaurant and asked for food. The same menu as the other place: goats' stew. "How long do we have to eat like this?" I wondered aloud. "This is just the beginning of your hardship," said Agnes. "It will get worse and worse as we cross the desert." My mind shook in surprise. "Are we going to cross the desert?" "Of course. We will only get a third of the story if we call it quits here." I hadn't thought of that.

Thankfully, although we were in a half Muslim country, they had plenty of beer. We talked, drank and as the sun went down made our way to the chief's house. He wanted to show us around. "This is where we are sleeping tonight." We were outside on a kind of terrace, with mats strewn across. "It's too hot to sleep inside. All you need is a sheet." He showed us the toilet — a hole in the ground surrounded by an opaque reed fence.

The wives came out of the house as the deep red sun moved below the horizon. They bedded down in a row. So did the chief. He indicated to us where to sleep, more or less next to him. We lay down and held hands and watched the stars. "Look," said Agnes, "the stars are more brilliant than in Tanzania." I leant over and kissed her and surreptitiously felt for her breast. We couldn't really make love with eight eyes around. I was too tired to be frustrated.

The sun, with its promise of another tortured day, woke us at six. One of the wives had already lit a fire and was stirring a pot of porridge. Another made the tea and the third served us. I didn't know what to think—the idea of three wives? That was a fantasy too far.

After breakfast we went out and strolled to our bar and ordered coffee—it was the instant type and there was no milk, but enough sugar to give us both immediate diabetes. The bar was empty apart from us and the owner. It looked as if it hadn't changed in a hundred years, apart from the ubiquitous Coca-Cola sign and another one advertising a Senegalese beer.

A couple of young men came in and I offered to buy them a coffee or beer if they preferred. They were a bit taken back by my out-of-nowhere hospitality but came and sat at our table. There was an uncomfortable silence. It seemed no one had anything to say. I decided to break the ice and asked them if they lived far away. One of them said "just round the corner, with my mother and father." "Is it hard to make a living here?" I questioned. This lit a spark. "So difficult. I want to get out of here. I've tried Dakar but it was hard going. But I saved up enough money to get myself to Paris." "Paris," Agnes took over from me. "That's a very long way to go." "I've got two cousins there so I won't be alone and they've promised to find me a job."

I interjected: "If all the young men leave here the town and the countryside the economy will go downhill. Without you working in the fields how will people eat?" "We men don't work in the fields. That's women's work." I could see Agnes grimace. "They look after the children and cook, eh? You men have a bad attitude. Yes, go to Paris. I see you don't do much here." The men were riled. "We hunt, some of us run a shop. And we have to mend our old cars and motorbikes, they are always breaking down." I had seen barely a dozen cars in the last 24 hours and there were only five or six little shops in the town. "Our wives like us to go—without the money we send back they wouldn't be able to buy nice clothes or repair the roof or build a good latrine or pay the school fees for our children."

The day passed. Sometimes we stopped men on the street. Sometimes we chatted in one of the bars. I suggested Agnes go off to talk to some of the women whilst I sat in the shade of the terrace of a bar and read some more Ben Okri.

After a while the conversations became boringly repetitive but we needed to know if there were any dissidents. Not one. Quite a few had done the journey already, spending two or three years in France. At least half of them wanted to do the journey again even though all of them had horror stories to tell — breakdowns in the desert, their driver losing his way, being manhandled by police in Spain whom the driver tried to pay off, sometimes with success, sometimes not, the awfulness of the abandoned, decrepit, unhygienic factory where they lived in Paris and the roughness of the French police who seemed to detest young immigrants — which prompted rioting in France in July this year after a policemen shot dead an innocent Tunisian teenager. Some had been arrested as they journeyed through Spain or France, incarcerated in prison for three months and then flown home by the authorities in a scary first plane ride, with little or no money in their pockets.

"The only way to get the full story is to ride with the traffickers," Agnes said again over lunch. "Do you have your passport?" "No, I thought this was as far as we were going." "Bloody hell. Fuck. Why on earth didn't you think we might go on? You are a total dimwit. One of us has to go back to Dakar and get it. I suppose it's in the hotel's safe box." It was the first time I had seen her angry. I offered to go. At least I would get a respite from the heat.

We asked in the café when the next train left. I'd just missed it. It was in two days' time. I said I'd hitch. But I hadn't noticed any cars or lorries that looked in good enough shape to cover that distance. We filled in the hours doing more interviews and trying to persuade the traffickers to make a date to take us. A white man had never been trafficked before and they took a lot of persuading. They bid us up to 50% more of what they had said yesterday.

The next morning I left Agnes feeling sad. She told me not to worry. There was plenty for her to do. She wanted to spend more time with the women to pull out of them more detail about how family life continued, while their men were away. What did they do without the (little) male help they counted on for heavy tasks, like mending the roof or cleaning the well. What did they spend the money on that their menfolk sent back from Europe?

I walked around the town, wondering if I'd find a vehicle. To my surprise, parked by our usual bar, there was a big oil tanker. I found the driver and he told me he delivered petrol to the small villages and towns along the southern rim of the desert. Now he was returning to Dakar.

He seemed happy to offer me a lift in return for €50. We drove sometimes on a track, sometimes on the barely marked sand but he seemed to know the route. Stupidly, because I couldn't find a larger container, I had filled up with water a small bottle I'd been given on the plane, nothing more. Needless to say, the heat was so dryly debilitating that within an hour or so I'd drunk it. I got more and more parched. I felt faint. The perspiration drooled down my face and body like quicksilver. The driver told me that in half an hour we would reach a small settlement by a river.

We did. I spied a little shop and I rushed in to see the glorious sight of a fridge. Inside was Coca-Cola. I drank three bottles with barely a breath between each glug. I bought four more for the journey.

I wandered around the village. I noticed all the houses had corrugated iron roofs, not thatch. All looked freshly painted. I saw a school. A simple one with small kids running around in the playground. Then at the end of the village was a mosque. Well-built, painted in white and shimmering in the sunlight. Down by the river women were bargaining for fresh fish. Women dressed as if their clothes were out of a fashion show. Ethereal damasks with radiant, colourful, scarves wound round their heads.

I returned to the bar where my driver was chatting to the owner. "How come everything looks so new and well-tended?" I asked. "Migrant money" replied the shop owner. "Every month the men in France send home a good chunk of what they have earned and this is how it goes."

We drove off. After six hours we reached the tarmac. Our conversation had long dried up. He'd told me he'd driven since dawn and now it was 3 o'clock and I could see his head was occasionally nodding. I offered to drive and then he could sleep. Surprisingly he welcomed the offer. He showed me how the gears worked. Eight forward gears and two backwards. Christ, I thought, what will I do if some kid runs out in the road, and I've got the weight of this enormous petrol tank behind me? How do I stop quickly?

I had no choice but to drive. If he'd gone on driving he would probably have fallen asleep at the wheel.

Once I'd shifted through most the gears and I was near the top one we were coasting along nicely. The driver fell asleep and I listened to a radio interview with Yousou N'Dour, the world-renowned Senegalese singer. It was followed by his songs, some my old favourites. He was warning people that once Senghor died there would be an attempt at a power grab by the army or some Big Man, as they are called in Africa. He implored his audience to come out on the street if that happened. They had to stand behind democracy. They had to improve the people's human rights. They had to push the government to invest more in the villages and countryside where most people still lived but whose political power was far less than those who lived in the towns and which got most of the money allocated by the government for infrastructure, health, education, water and electricity. The lyrics were very to the point, the melody captivating, beguiling, and his voice rich and deep.

The driver was now awake. As we approached Dakar he said he should take over. I never got a chance to try the reverse gears but I was exhilarated by my experience. The endorphins were jumping as if I'd jogged for an hour.

He dropped me off by a taxi stand. I was driven to the hotel. Madame Chevalier was as welcoming as before. I had a couple of cold beers and settled down to eat a rabbit stew with a very good French red wine. I checked that my passport was still in the safe and went upstairs to my room and fell instantly asleep, my body exhausted by the heat and the long journey.

I had to wait for two days before the next train left. I wandered around missing Agnes and thinking half a week has nearly passed and I'd only made love to her once.

Then I had the bright idea to go to the university and asked around if anyone had done a study of the migrant traffic. I stopped first at the economics department, found one of the lecturers and was directed to the social studies department where there was a migration unit. There were four of them and they explained they had a UN grant for two years. They had uncovered a lot of valuable information. They had estimates of the numbers who had crossed the Sahara to Morocco for each of the last five years. They had done hundreds of interviews and had a rough and ready list of the traffickers who seemed reasonably honest and those who had a reputation for short cuts, exploitation and thuggery. None of the researchers had actually travelled across the desert but they had a pretty good idea of where the traffickers crossed the Moroccan border and the route they took through Morocco to avoid the police.

A day and a half later I was on the night train, lying in bed without Agnes. My heart truly ached. My body shook with anticipation as I imagined what would happen when we could find some time to be private and alone. I wondered if I'd live so intensely again.

I got myself into our town in one of the donkey carts and went straight to the chief's house. I expected to find Agnes there as it was only seven in the morning. I knocked. A wife opened the door and took me to where the chief was having his morning tea. After the usual very polite greetings he gave me a letter. It was from Agnes. She said she'd got bored waiting for me. She'd been offered a ride by a trafficker who seemed very trustworthy. She had thought that since he wasn't over-packing his lorry and that there were many cans of water she wanted to get going. Maybe, she wrote, it will take you a week to find another good man. Let's meet up, she suggested, in Casablanca at that bar where they made that famous film "Casablanca."

I was stunned. It didn't make sense. There was no endearment at the end of the letter. Not even a signature. I just couldn't believe she had not waited for me. She hadn't struck me as a woman who would take that kind of risk all alone. "Where did you get the letter?" I asked the chief. "A boy brought it. He said he worked at the bar. A man had dropped it off."

"This can't be Agnes," I said, panicked. I could barely hold back my tears. I was almost breathless. My voice became strangulated — a frightful feeling of impotence and despair. "What should I do?" I asked the chief. The chief was calm and collected. "Let's walk down to the bar and see if we can find out more about the man who dropped the letter off."

"Yes, I recognise the guy. I see him hanging out with the traffickers," said the owner of the bar. "But he often drinks somewhere else."

Armed with a rough and ready description of the man we set out to visit the other bars in town. By now I knew it was the traffickers who had taken Agnes away by either guile or force, probably the latter, given the way the letter was written. It must have been a trafficker with some experience since the writer had probably heard of the old film "Casablanca." I presume they had, at the least, slapped her around to get that information out of her.

At the third bar-cum-café we hit lucky. The chief was respected, and few people dared lie or mislead him. The owner did not prevaricate. "Jonas Makumi is his name. He's often here when he is not taking a load of migrants across the desert. He's been doing it for years. But I haven't seen him for three or four days. I guess he's on a trip." "Do you think he could have kidnapped Agnes?" I asked the chief. "I've heard beside the usual migration the traffickers are now getting into the sex trade," he replied, shaking his head. "Merde, what is it all coming to?"

"Just the last few months I've been hearing more and more about it. They go into the villages and pretend to be bringing young girls to a new boarding school in the town. The villagers are innocent and hand over their daughters." I looked appalled. I was in shock. "Why don't you go and talk to the Imam. Sometimes they hear about everything."

Sex trade. Christ, that would be the most terrible and horrifying thing. I had no idea from my earlier life that evil could multiply itself so fast. Who could I appeal to for help? There was no Tanzanian embassy here and probably none in Morocco.

My shirt was drenched with sweat. I was shaking. I had to sit down. The chief could see I was hyperventilating. He ordered us a Coke. The right drink in this situation, even though I detested the impact of the western soft drink industry in Africa.

"Where would they traffic her to?" I asked the chief and the bar owner. They shrugged. "Have you no idea where they could sell her?" My voice rose, quavering. The chief took his hat off, scratching his scalp. "If I had to take a guess, I would say Mauritania, the country that lies between us and Morocco. It's very, very poor.

Not many people. It lives under the shadow of Morocco. It still has slavery. I've heard that on the radio."

"So if he was taking a load of migrants to Morocco he could stop off in Mauritania and find a slave dealer to buy Agnes. But by now he will have done that and will have another $3,000 in his pocket."

"What would a slave be made to do, chief?" "A maid for a rich family, a concubine for a chief, if she were lucky. If she were unlucky, working 12 hours a day in a phosphate mine and being raped regularly by the male workers. Or being a full-time member of a brothel, locked in night and day. No pay for anything."

"You know all this?" I asked. "One of my nieces was hijacked and then raped. I paid off some officials and got her out. She's now a local weaver. A lovely girl but she has never got over the degradation. She is always depressed. I doubt if she will find a husband in this state."

"I'm going to go tomorrow, find Agnes and pay someone off," I almost shouted. "It will be harder for you than it was for me," said the chief, "Mauritania is the poorest country in the old French empire. There was only sand until they found phosphate some years ago.

The French invested almost nothing. They are primitives. Arabs, Ugh." He grimaced. "Neither Morocco nor Senegal wanted to take the country on. Only very few speak French and you don't know the local languages."

"Sleep on it," the chief advised. "Go and buy some beer and we will put it in the fridge to cool before dinner." He walked away and then turned. He had another thought. "I don't know if it would help but if you want you can sleep with my third wife tonight."

Not a good idea, I thought. Tempting though it would be to get close to the body of a soothing woman, I felt I was given to Agnes and that was that. I tried to explain my thinking to him but he just smiled. Probably he thought I was being a bit stupid since this was a great honour he was bestowing on me. He didn't extend hospitality like this every day.

I walked back with him. He suggested I should rest. I took out my book and tried to read. More Ben Okri: "It is only when the diverse peoples of the earth meet and learn from and love one another that we can begin to get an inkling of this awesome picture. Call it the picture of divinity, or humanity if you want, but like the magic powder that Africans sometime allude to this great picture has been distributed amongst all of us; and one aspect of our destiny on earth may be to discover something of that grand image or music of our collective souls, of our immense possibilities, of our infinite riches. No one person or people has found the final road or the great keyboard or exclusive expression of this jigsaw of humanity. Only together, as one people of the earth, facing our common predicament and redeeming fire, can we make use of the universal gift, this map of our earthly journey and glory." How true right here and right now, I thought. The heat soon had me dozing and then sleeping. I woke up in time for a beer before dinner.

We ate and drank—only a little for the chief—a lot for me. He told us stories of his father and grandfather, chiefs before him who had had to kowtow before the French. "They landed us with taxes and all sorts of regulations. They tried to shut down our weaving industry so they could sell French-made clothes. If we disobeyed they put us in prison, often in solitary confinement. We never had prisons before the French came. A beating on the back and a shaming were enough to punish evildoers."

The sun goes down early in the tropics. All day the sun had been remorseless. I wanted to escape the waning rays of a very long day. We went to our beds on the sheltered veranda. The chief indicated I lie on the mattress closest to his third wife. She took my hand and stroked my face. I let her do that until I fell asleep.

I woke up as the sun rose. I knew what I had to do, despite the dangers. This time I bought a big water bottle and some bananas and cheese. The little store stocked eggs which I would hard boil and its own baguettes. Well, I thought once again, French occupation had done some good! I went to say goodbye to the chief and to boil the eggs. I shoved it all in my rucksack and found a donkey cart to take me to the border post between Senegal and Mauritania. I hired a canoe to ferry me over the river. I wanted to be independent of the traffickers so I'd decided to hitch.

The customs men, one Senegalese, the other Mauritanian, looked at my passport and then talked to each other. They were curious, I guess. This was probably the first time they'd met a white traveller. I told them I'd been staying with the chief and that I was trying to get to the capital, Nouakchott, where a Mauritanian friend I'd met at university lived and was now in the ministry of foreign affairs, working in the foreign minister's office. This seemed to impress them. They each stamped my passport and asked for a bribe. I gave each of them €10 and asked if I could sit in the shade under their lean-to. It was incredibly hot—at least 40ºC. I wilted and waited and drank. They had told me that perhaps once a day a truck carrying peanuts came through.

Nothing appeared. I sat there all day, drifting into depression. My world seemed to have become blank and naked and drained of colour, sepia-toned in fact. I looked at the sand. It stretched to the horizon, an unchanging, enduring, yellow-brown. The French explorer, Bagnold, wrote of how "The grooves and the corrugated sand resemble the hollow of the roof of a dog's mouth." From time to time there was a dried-out rivulet. I suppose every couple of years it must rain for an hour or two. Christ, how long can I keep myself going? The time crept by. I ate some of the bananas and cheese. I feared the next few days, across the empty, water-starved, desert. It loomed in my mind large and foreboding like a great cloud, coloured a dark brownie yellow, a smog, absorbing the colour of the sand dunes.

Conversation was not to be had with the border guards. Occasionally they talked to each other or to the rare donkey cart driver passing through, which made me think there must be a village ahead. I decided to try and hitch a lift on the next one. At least I'd feel the satisfaction of being on my way. Two hours later one arrived. I talked to the driver, offered him €10 and we were off at a slow jog. More and more sand. The occasional shrub became the very occasional shrub. Not even a goat.

An hour later we arrived at a settlement. There were a few palm trees around a water hole. I assumed there was a spring. There were some desert grasses which a few goats grazed on. There were even some chickens. I counted half a dozen camels. There was a little shop. I went in. Coca-Cola had been here before me — there was a fridge in the corner. I wondered how far the Coca-Cola delivery vans penetrated into the desert. Perhaps that would be my next lift. I couldn't see any source of income in the village. Perhaps they bred camels and sold them in Senegal. I suppose they had a couple of the young men sending back money from the north.

In our bad French the donkey driver and I had chatted a little. I asked him where I could stay. He offered his home. There was a spare bed. His son was away in France. He told me later that his son had bought him the donkey cart. There were only fifteen of them in the village. He had just come back from selling goat and camel meat to the town where I'd stayed and had returned with maize, peanuts, some cans of fish and beans, and a big box of aspirins. I tried to imagine what happened when there was a real illness—appendicitis, a stroke, a serious infection. Aspirins were no good for that. How privileged we are. Couldn't we in the richer countries make sure, if nothing else, that every poor village in the world had a good stock of basic medicines, carefully labelled for what they could help with? I'd read that morphine was not available to one-third of the world's people. People like this confronting an excruciating, painful death from cancer or kidney failure have only local remedies to give them relief. Sometimes they work—maybe the placebo effect. More often they don't. We can die from a thousand cuts, I thought, we can die from a serious illness, we can die from jealously but here you could die if you had a small accident. I thought of a cart's wheel running over a foot and causing a gash, gangrene setting in, and a painful death following.

It was another evening with nothing to do but gaze at the stars and read my Ben Okri novel by the light of the single lantern. Over the high hills of distant sand dunes the pale moon was sailing, growing more brilliant as the western horizon lost its colour.

I'd been fed on maize porridge and tinned beans. I took a chance with the spring water. I felt a bit better. But deep inside I was craving, weeping for Agnes. My heart felt empty. I was in a desolate place, a dehydrated desert around me. An intimation of emptiness.

I was wakened by my host. "You are in luck. A peanut truck has just arrived. I've talked to him. He'll take you. He's going all the way to the capital. It's a two-day journey to Nouakchott and he'll drive straight through. There's no sizeable village and nowhere to sleep." I could see it was going to be a grim trip. I negotiated a fee of €50 and climbed in beside him. It was all flat expanse and wide sky. Only the rare dune broke up the monotony.

After half a day the driver pulled up. "Let's eat and then sleep. We can sleep in the shade under the lorry." For hours, I'd been feeling the sweat rolling down my face and neck like balls of quicksilver. I pulled out my French meal, which he declined. He had his own porridge wrapped in a plastic bag. I shared a banana with him. We crawled under the lorry and I immediately fell asleep. I've no idea for how long but we both sat up as we heard the sound of a lorry coming close. It stopped. It was empty apart from a driver and his mate.

My driver whispered to me, "I think these are traffickers on their way home." They were obviously father and son. I told them I was a journalist and was writing about the Sahara and who could make a living in this dried-out wilderness. Would they talk to me for my article? I added that if they wanted me to change their names I would.

We climbed into the tarpaulin-covered back of their lorry, shielded from the ever-blazing sun, and started to talk.

They told me they had been driving backwards and forwards to Morocco and the Mediterranean shore for five years. They took migrants and it was a very good business. In Tangier they handed their cargo over to Spanish traffickers. They lived in a town in Senegal further down the line than Bakel. The older one said,

"I've built a big house there. Besides this lorry, I have a new Citroen. I pay for my children to go to boarding school in Dakar." "How many wives do you have?" I asked. "Four." He was obviously richer than my friend the chief.

"Where have you come from on this journey," I asked. "From the Mauritanian-Moroccan border," the father said. "We are so tired. We want to get home today."

I summoned up my courage. "Did you see going north a lorry with a young woman?" "Yes, I quite often see a woman or two. Women go up north to earn money cooking for the men. So there are usually one or two on each lorry, I think we passed about three lorries on this trip." I realised I wasn't going to get intelligence on Agnes's trail if this was the case. For the first time I wished she were white and would stand out.

The peanut trader and I continued our northern journey. At sunset we dismounted. I could see the curve of the moon, breathlessly beautiful in the crystal-clear sky; it had a halo around it. We both had our simple rations. Satisfied, we slept under the lorry again.

In the night a vicious wind blew up. The sand seemed to be trying to enter deep into my body, pushing to find a way in through my ears, nostrils and mouth. I turned my back to the wind and put my shirt over my head. Hassanein Bey wrote a dramatic account of such a storm: "It is though the surface were underlaid with steampipes, with thousands of orifices through which tiny jets of steam are puffing out. The sand leaps in little spurts and whirls. Inch by inch the disturbance rises as the wind increases its force. It seems though the whole surface of the desert were rising in obedience to some up thrusting force beneath. Larger pebbles strike against the knees, the shins, the thighs. The sand-grains climb the body till it strikes the face and goes over the head. The sky is shut out, all but the nearest objects fade from view, the universe is filled."

In the morning the track had disappeared. The wind still blew and the grit even penetrated the lorry's cabin. "I've got GPS," said the driver, "But we will have to wait for the storm to blow over. I can't get a signal. I can't see out of the window." We sat there for most of the day, tasting the grit and spitting it out. Finally, towards evening the storm mellowed, then abated. We set off, hoping to get in two hours of driving before nightfall. There was no sign of a track. Even with the

GPS it could not help us find the track even if our direction was right. I realized there would be little chance of meeting someone coming the other way.

The next day we found a road and then small villages. Eventually we hit a tarred road and a signpost saying Nouakchott, 50 kilometres. Before long we were in the town.

Until 1958 it was just a village. But after independence from France it grew fast and now it harbours around 700,000 souls. It houses one-sixth of the country's population of four million. Whole villages have been abandoned as people are hit by droughts and increasing desertification, and families migrate to the city. Inevitably shanty towns have grown up and spread their tentacles right through the city. Half of the population lives in tents and shacks. The city lies close to the Atlantic and is threatened by sand dunes moving in to join up with the desert. Thanks to global warming the rising water level of the Atlantic means that there is often flooding. The drains get blocked and the sewers overflow. It becomes full of stinking ponds. Many say it will be uninhabitable before long and the whole city should be moved inland.

It reminded me of Rudyard Kipling's poem about Calcutta:

"As the fungus sprouts chaotic from its bed,
So it spread-
Chance-directed, chance-erected, laid and built
On the silt-
Palace, byre, hovel — poverty and pride-
Side by side;
And, above the packed and pestilential town,
Death looked down."

The only thing that saves the country's economy are the large reserves of iron ore, copper, potash, gold and gypsum. They provide half of the country's export earnings. There are rich fishing areas off the continental shelf.

I'd picked up an internet connection for the first time since I began my journey. I came across a British Foreign Office site that made my heart sink. It warned British people not to travel to the country. It read: "Terrorists are likely to try to carry out attacks, including kidnapping. You should be especially vigilant in public places. Attacks could be indiscriminate, including in places visited by foreigners. The terrorists mainly come from Al-Qaeda in the Islamic Maghreb and Polisario. Slavery, female genital mutilation, child labour and human trafficking are common." The injustice of it all appalled me. My throat tightened. Tears edged through my eyelashes as I thought of my Agnes, captured and bound.

The driver now found a signal for his radio. I tuned it into the BBC short wave World Service. It was news time: Brexit and the rise of Prime Minister Boris Johnson, Trump's latest military mess-up with Iran and then, to my surprise, a third item about migrants who had crossed the Sahara on the same route as us and who had tried to cross the Mediterranean at its narrowest point: "Bathers in a southern Spanish beach near Cadiz, eight miles from the coast of North Africa, watched in amazement when a large dinghy carrying as many as 20 African migrants came ashore in broad daylight before its occupants fled into the surrounding countryside. The Spanish coastguard had earlier received an SOS call from another dinghy and rescued all eight people on board. The Moroccan navy rescued seven people from another vessel."

According to the EU's Frontex, its border agency, I later learned, 7,500 immigrants had made the crossing to

Spain in the first three months of this year, compared with 3,600 in the same period last year. In June alone, 2,200 attempted to cross the strait on vessels ranging from inflatable toy boats to high powered launches piloted by trafficker.

I parted company with the driver in the town centre and asked a passer-by for directions to an hotel. I needed the accoutrements of some luxury after that drive—a bathroom that worked for starters.

When I checked in at the desk I spied a pile of newspapers. There was an International Herald Tribune flown in from Paris, albeit two days old. Up in my room, showered, clean and changed I opened it. To my surprise there was an article on the Sahara migrants. Suddenly I was being swamped by reports on migrants. The South African editor had pushed us in the right direction. Here was a good story for us, if not for the migrants:

"When smugglers believe there are police or military in the area, or if they have technical problems because of the great hazards of the desert tracks, they have taken to kicking the migrants out of their vehicles and leaving them to fend for themselves, without water, food or shelter, aid workers report. Already this year, the local government and the United Nations have rescued[1] at least 1,000 migrants who were left stranded by traffickers. But the UN counts only people it finds alive; the number of those who died of thirst in temperatures that can reach over 110°F (40°C) is unknown, but likely exceeds the number of those rescued. Aid workers say this is the most dangerous year yet for these migrants."

Was Agnes abandoned in the desert? The thought turned me to ice. Reality, imperturbable, forbidding and sickening, plunged deep into the nether regions of my stomach. I felt an incompetent fool. I tried to be rational. If she was, then I didn't think there was much I could do. The sensible thing was to continue to Casablanca and go to the hotel of the famous, iconoclastic film, where we had said long ago we would rendezvous if we ever got separated. In my Nouakchott hotel the receptionist let me look at a map of northwest Africa.

There was a road of sorts, tarred but potholed in a worn-out kind of way, she informed me, that went up the coast. There were even buses that plied the route. It

---

[1] https://www.iom.int/news/un-migration-agency-search-and-rescue-missions-sahara-desert-help-1000-migrants

looked like it was a 1,500-kilometre journey. My head was full of doubts. Maybe Agnes had been trafficked and was being used as a concubine somewhere in Nouakchott. Thoughts like this went round and round in my head. They got nowhere. I felt dazed, limp, disembodied, horribly isolated and lonely.

I walked around the town in an attempt to calm down and think it out. There were some substantial buildings — banks, government buildings, the offices of oil and mining companies, of the local airline, Air France and Air Maroc. In between a handful of restaurants offering in the main Moroccan food. But not much more. A hundred metres from the central square the shanty towns began. I wandered down a lane: mud-built houses, a ditch for the sewerage to collect, excrement and plastic bags intermingled, the occasional standpipe for water, little shops including a pharmacist with not more than a dozen different medicines and a box of condoms. Children were playing with hoops, skipping with ropes, some playing football and others sitting outside their houses looking listless. I felt a message was being drummed into me: there is no escape from the hard things of this world, neither for them nor for me, the materially spoilt observer...

... Somehow, I had made it to the Casablanca hotel. I asked the desk about Agnes. I described her and only got shakes of the head. A poignant horror of sensation shivered through me. I felt my hands shaking. I pulled myself together and asked when the new shift came on. I checked in, showered, washed my very dirty, sand-filled hair and my underpants and then went down to find a place on the terrace and ordered a Campari. How nice to have something other than beer. I scanned the crowd at what is still obviously a very popular place among the better-to-do. There was a new Sam. He was good. The music soothed me.

What could I do but wait? I wanted to go for a walk after all those days cramped up in buses. I felt I didn't dare. I didn't want to miss Agnes if she was around. I pulled my book out and realized there were only a dozen pages left. Tomorrow I'd have to see if there was an English-language bookshop in town. I finished it, wandered into the lobby, asked the new shift the same question, got the same answer and found Le Monde, El País and some local papers. I ordered a bottle of Moroccan red wine. Not so bad. I remember my parents used to drink it decades ago. Our neighbour who often visited Morocco told us that quite a number of Moroccans drink publicly, even though they are Muslims.

It was all very beguiling. If it wasn't for the pain in my stomach and the anxiety that rested in my brain I would have enjoyed the languid, lackadaisical, atmosphere. The big room with its stage and upright piano was still as I remembered it from the film. Tonight there were only a few people at the tables. The waiters and waitresses were having an easy time. I wanted it to fill up, for Sam to sing and for Agnes to walk through the door.

I drank a couple of glasses, concentrated on the local French-language paper and tried to take my mind off it all. I looked up to see a woman, perhaps in her late twenties, two tables away looking at me. She gave me a small smile. I went on reading. Then I got bored and put the paper down. She was looking at me again. She looked Spanish. She smiled and I smiled back. She stood up and came over. "I'm Maria. I'm from Madrid. Let me buy you a drink. I know the best wines here." I was a bit flummoxed by her audacity. But also amused. Why not, I thought. I asked her what she was doing here. "I'm a journalist for El País, working on a story about child kidnapping and trafficking by Spanish criminals." "I'm a journalist too." "I'm not surprised. We always sniff each other out." "Our police have been on the issue for years but they don't seem able to crack it. Just an arrest here and an arrest there. The kingpins never get touched." I couldn't believe I'd met another journalist — hence her lack of inhibition about stepping forward and offering me a drink — and one with a similar interest to mine.

We talked. We ordered dinner and I realized how hungry I was now I had some alcohol in my veins. Like all good journalists she had quite a capacity for booze.

It was a gently warm evening — quite unlike the desert that went from hot to cold in minutes. We sat outside. The sun gradually dipped, flaming yellow and red, below the horizon. The western sky was full of a murky orange glow glittering with a few feathers of pale cloud. I felt as if the night was broadcasting the heat of my sorrow. We swapped stories. She had unearthed some important leads. She was hell-bent on plumbing the depths of her story, even though she knew that the nearer she got to the mafia bosses the more dangerous life would become. I asked her if she thought these child traffickers also handled young adult women like Agnes. She was sure they did.

By ten o'clock the drink had taken a toll on both of us. We agreed it was time to go up to our rooms, get some sleep and meet at eight for breakfast. A bit the worse for wear I wrapped my arms around her, held her and kissed the top of her head. She didn't seem to mind. We headed for the lifts. I felt good that I now had a colleague who I could talk to and get advice. She obviously had an intimate knowledge of the country. And she was so pretty, all sweetness and abundance: curves, dark eyes and kissable lips.

Breakfast was a mind-opener. She told me how the traffickers worked through kidnapping and how they managed to "place" the young girls and women in brothels and factories. "In countries like Thailand and the Philippines the supply of local girls is sufficient, but in Africa, Europe, Latin America and America there are never enough," Maria explained. "It is so easy to intimidate them. They take their ID away. They give them a little taste of torture if they misbehave so they know what will happen if they try to escape. They give them a tiny amount of money and once a month they can make a list of what they want to spend it on — shampoo, lipstick, a dress or even the Bible or Koran. Then one of the guards goes off to buy them. They have to think themselves lucky."

"I think I'm in the right country to find the masterminds. It's a weird country. Its economy is quite good. It has a king with a great deal of power. It also has a parliament which gives its members quite a lot of latitude. But the big sensitive questions land on the king's desk.

You don't feel that sense of repression or being watched that you get in many Arab countries. The corruption in business is much less. The police are less corrupt and less violent and the news media have quite a bit of freedom. Because it's more open it's easier to gather information." I asked Maria if she'd fathomed why Morocco produces so many of the terrorist bombers in Europe and why these kidnapping gangs are produced here. "There must be some major dislocation in the society but I can't explain it more."

"What should I do?" I asked. "Stay here or go back to Mauritania?" She got up to go to the bathroom and I wondered what she was thinking. When she returned she gave me a slow smile. I could see she had an intelligent face, quizzical, a large brow, her eyes and hair almost black. A sense of curiosity marked her out. The hair was pushed well back and tied at the nape of the neck. "Look, Jon, the newspaper says I have to wrap this story in a week. The editor says he can't pay me indefinitely to work on one story. So what I propose is that you help me with this one of mine and then, I've got two week's holiday that I'm owed, I'll help you." It seemed it was an offer too good to be true. We did a high five and ordered another cup of coffee.

She briefed me on what she knew. "I'm certain their base of operations is Casablanca. It's the country's biggest city with the biggest slums. It's the main port and ships go in and out of here night and day all over the world. Smuggling girls inside containers is relatively easy. They bring them in from far and wide, lie low with them in the city for a week or so until the fuss about their disappearance has died down and then ship them out to wherever they've been 'placed'." "So it's a constant flow," I asked? "More or less. If I think too hard about it it makes me sick in my gut," she added, a painful grimace on her face.

"The regime has an interest in not drawing attention to this business. Not necessarily because it's corrupt, even though some officials and police officers may be, but because they want Morocco's bad side to have a low profile. This is a big tourist country. The government prefers for the tourists going to the beach towns or Marrakesh to be unaware of this part of life. This is one of the things that the news media are not allowed to report on."

It was almost eleven by the time Maria had emptied out what she knew. It was time for another coffee and then a stroll round the hotel's extensive garden, replete with birds of paradise, bougainvillea and flowering cacti. I was flummoxed as to how she and I could break into this wall of silence and, eventually, get the gang leaders behind bars, if not here, in Europe.

"The media may not report the story," she continued. "But that doesn't mean that individual journalists don't know about it and have some insights into how it works. They'll talk to us if we can find them. They are frustrated. I think we should start there."

"I've got a bright idea," I interjected. "Let's pretend we are doing a story about the Casablanca film and that we want to find out if Moroccans themselves still know about it. If we approach enough of the French-language newspapers, radio and TV stations we are bound to find someone who both knows about the film and also knows a colleague who has some sort of interest or knowledge in what we are after."

"Brilliant," Maria said. "Let's go and search the net." We divided up the media, went up to our rooms, searched the net for phone numbers and started dialling newsrooms. It was easy. After an hour I knocked on her door and we went down to lunch. "I've made three appointments, two for this evening," I said. "And I've made two," Maria added. "Mine are for tomorrow, so why don't I come with you this evening?"

I badly wanted a walk and also to see a bit of the town. We had a few hours before we started work. Maria wove her way through the small, dirty streets and alleyways. What a cacophony of constant noise — it far exceeded what I'd experienced in black Africa. "We are heading for the docks so we can see them in daylight," she said. "I'm pretty sure they ship these girls out hidden in containers."

Maria talked on. I was distracted by my thoughts. Was I wasting a precious week? Shouldn't I go off on my own? No, this was right. She was far more experienced than me. I carried my pain about Agnes deep down in my stomach. I just had to live with it. I continued walking beside Maria. I picked up again on what she was saying.

"A few years ago I wrote a story about child labour in carpet factories in Morocco, prompted by a report by the Anti-Slavery Society in London — an interesting, reliable outfit, that is a direct descendent of Wilberforce's successful campaign to abolish slavery in the British Empire. Of course, child labour, drawing in kids from eight to sixteen or so from local villages, is not the same as the international trafficking of older girls and young women. But this is how I got interested in trafficking. The subject kept cropping up."

We walked on. The docks were surrounded by a high fence with barbed wire at the top. "There are ways in," explained Maria. "The easiest is bribes for the gatekeepers, late at night when nobody else is around and there may be only two guys in charge. I guess they don't even see the girls — they arrive in vans with the windows darkened. They probably assume it's drug traffickers shipping stuff to Europe. They don't feel they should have a conscience about letting these men through. This was Europe's problem where people shopped for the stuff. Without the shoppers there wouldn't be a drug trade." "I agree," I said. "It's our end that are the sinners and criminals. I'd lock up these smokers, injectors and snorters. You know in America they lock up the black young men on the street who are trading small amounts of this stuff and ignore the well-educated, mainly white, middle and upper class who consume it." "So you understand," continued Maria, "if these guards think it's drug traffickers, not girls, they are letting through, they more or less say, 'good luck to you'. Of course, they like the bribe too."

"Time to find a taxi. We must get back pronto to the town centre. You have your first appointment in half an hour. I'll come with you. Later I'll take you to a local place for dinner. The food is more interesting and cheaper. I've got to save up for a bribe," she said, laughing. Her smile worked on me. Also her idealism and determination. God, I thought. I've already got one pretty woman on my brain. Please not a second. If I'm not careful I'll end up like that chief we stayed with. Let's hope she has a boyfriend or husband back in Madrid whom she loves very much.

Maria told me, as the taxi navigated the crowded traffic and narrow streets, that she had a source who had given her this idea of inspecting the docks. Journalists don't usually give money in return for information.

But, as she explained, in this case it might be necessary. This was an important enough story to justify it. The guards would have to be bribed. But she would also try and talk to them and explain what she believed was really going on. That might make the bribe less. The newspaper wouldn't give her money for this purpose up front, but she thought if she got the story they might cough up later. So she was going to risk using her own money.

I realized Maria was a rather special woman. She not only had drive, she had a moral compass too. That's the kind of journalist I wanted to be.

"Anyway," she said, "we need to get more info before we risk a visit inside the docks. Let's hope these Moroccan journalists give us some good thoughts." We ended up interviewing three journalists that evening, passed on by the two editors of the culture pages to whom we chatted about the old film. They were the ones who specialised in crime. Somewhat to our surprise all of them confirmed Maria's hunch. "But why don't you run these stories? Why don't you make it a national scandal?" She tried to pin them down one by one.

It was tough going. Two were just evasive, saying that with the crime rate and corruption increasing all the time they had their work cut out dealing with shady banks and businesses, money laundering and corrupt policemen.

But the third, a young man with a brightly lit face and a toothy smile, was obviously a computer geek. "I only joined the paper earlier this year so I'm still working as an intern. The big stories are given to the older journalists so often I have time on my hands. So I've done some research myself on trafficking. If you look at police records arrests for prostitution in say, Chile, Uruguay, the US, Canada, Spain and Denmark for instance you will see that around half the girls are Moroccan. I don't know why so many should come from here. Maybe it's just by chance because of some particularly clever and well-organised mafia-types." "Yes," I said, "I can't understand either why so many terrorists exploding these bombs in Europe come from Morocco. Is there something badly wrong with this society that other developing countries don't suffer from as much?"

"I've wracked my head about this. I've talked to some colleagues. I've talked to my old professor of social science. I even talked to my Imam, but nobody is sure.

The nearest I've come to an explanation is the argument that the traffickers are ex-army and have served in the army fighting the Polisario. The government and the army are determined to use any means, fair and foul, to hold on to the territory. So officers encourage their soldiers to shoot on sight, to burn villages if they think they are hiding guerrillas, and to intimidate the populace by raping the women. So when their two years of military service are over and they return to Morocco proper they miss the wildness of their army adventures. They have no respect for women. They want nothing better than to find another target to blow up and are easy recruiting material for Al Qaeda or the trafficking gangs — which allow them to have as many girls or women as they want to have. They shed their morality in Western Sahara."

We headed off to Agnes's eating joint — well, not really a joint, it was a small, but nicely furnished restaurant on a back street with the pleasant smell of an atmosphere left by decades of customers eating good food. We ate couscous and oven-baked chicken and drank a good deal of red wine. We even found there was a Moroccan-made brandy. It was a bit rough, but not bad considering it was an Islamic country. We finished off dinner with that.

"I think that young journalist is really on the ball," said Marie. "I do too. It makes sense to me. We are going to interview these other journalists tomorrow, but I doubt if we will come up with a better explanation."

"OK, Marie said, "that was a great meal and a good day's work. Let me pay the bill and we'll go." We walked to the hotel trying to shake off the haze of alcohol that enveloped both of us. Outside her room, she asked me if I'd like one more brandy out of the mini bar. It was difficult to refuse. She poured them out and then kissed me. My senses went haywire, and I couldn't stop myself. I was seized by lust. The lunacy of love, I thought? Maybe. But I wanted it too. Agnes disappeared into the haze. Afterwards as we lolled on the bed, having found the unfinished brandies, I told her it was only the second time in my life I'd made love. I started to tell her about Agnes and me but I couldn't keep my eyes open. My last thought was that she was wanton but not wicked. She wouldn't make me pay a price with Agnes for these moments of passion. I wrapped my arms around her and fell asleep. When I woke as the crystal light of early morning penetrated into the room, my first thought was, was yesterday true? It had been an unbelievable day. But I was more than aware I'd landed myself into the soup by making love to Maria. Would she help me find Agnes now? It was all becoming too complicated. My brain vaulted between euphoria and fear. A bittersweet start to the day. I looked at Maria, still sleeping. Maybe I'd blown it. Would she want to help me find a rival?

I left her a note to say I'd gone downstairs for breakfast. Half an hour later a rested and cheerful Maria joined me. She put her arm around my neck and whispered: "It was beautiful, but never again," she said. "We are working together to find one of the two women you are drawn to. That's enough. In fact, it's one too many!" We both laughed. I was relieved. I was a novice, green all through. I was out of my depth in the passion world. I hadn't realized how complicated it can be. Learning about the intricacies and intrigues of love was something yet to come into my life. I was at stage number one, just out of the box. A puppy. Later I came to realize that many girls are pretty and a few beautiful. But like gorgeous flowers I didn't need to pick them to enjoy them. It was better on emotional stability that way.

We jumped into a taxi and drove to our next appointments. It was more or less the same story as yesterday evening although one journalist emphasised that he was pretty sure some rather high-ranking policemen were being paid off. It wasn't just the guards on the gates of the docks.

All of the journalists seemed glad we were working on the story. If you publish it in Spain it will make it easier for us to write about it, they said. They told us to come back if we got stuck.

"So where do we go next?" I asked Maria. "Let's have a coffee and think," as she pointed out a coffee bar. I was beginning to feel that there was no escape from the hard feelings and doings of this world. At this stage only Maria's exuberance and single-minded methodology could raise my spirits.

Maria was upbeat: "My idea is that we work backwards. We start at the docks. First, we get the licence plate numbers. Then we go to the car registration office and ask to see who owns the van. If they refuse to give the name and address the bribe to change their mind won't be all that much!"

For two evenings we monitored the traffic that went through the dock gate, waiting for a van with darkened glass. It gets cold in the late evening even if it is Africa. We shivered. Although the sky was dense with cloud a diffused light from some fragment of the moon helped us see. The scent of thousands of wooden crates loaded and impregnated with oranges and lemons hung in the air as they rested on the dockside to be loaded onto ships the next morning. Half a dozen lorries came, unloaded their goods next to a ship and drove off. The one essential was to wait. The minutes dragged themselves by, and then the hours. There was no van with darkened glass. But the second evening it came. We'd already handed the guard we had talked to some money and he waved us through. We ran after the van, keeping in the shadows. Thirty or so metres on, the van pulled into a badly lit corner and out tumbled twelve girls, maybe 16, maybe 18 years old and one or two older. It was hard to see them in the gloom. They were frog-marched by two men onto a nearby ship loaded with large containers. We lost sight of them but could hear the cries and sobbing of the girls and then the clanging of a steel door. A moment passed. A wall of silence descended. We looked at each other. We both shrugged, our faces grey in the murky light. What was going to happen next? I was suddenly frightened, not for myself but for the girls — and Agnes if she was there too.

Maria scribbled down the number plate details and we waited until the van left and made our way back to the hotel. The next day at nine sharp we were at the motor registration office. The money did the trick and soon we had a name and address of the van owner — and the bonus of good directions to it from the man at the desk.

Again, it was time for a coffee and more thought. "We can't just roll up to the house," I said. "Of course not. The best thing is to wait some discrete distance away and see who comes out and in. Then it will be easier for me, a woman, than the two of us, to walk up casually to a guard who is on his own, who looks less educated and therefore more susceptible to a bribe and try and get him to talk." "But what on earth are you going to say?" I asked.

"Yes, what should I say? No, that idea is not so good. Let me have a think." For two or three minutes or so I people-watched, counting the women who didn't wear a head covering of some sort. I reckoned it was 10 out of 30, not bad, I thought, for a Muslim country these days. "I've got it," Maria raised her voice a tone. "They're bound to have a maid or a cook. Perhaps the wife or sister of one of the guys. Either this woman is bribed to keep her eyes closed or she is intimidated by the men, even beaten." "The fulcrum is female!" I shouted, jesting. "You've got it! If we get to the house early in the morning we can intercept her on the way to work." "But leave that to me. You will just frighten her." "So what do I do?" "You just sit in the car and if I have to make a run for it you'll be ready for me."

"Let's hire the car now," Maria said. "We've not got much to do now until tomorrow morning. I'll take you to the sea. It's not far." The beach was almost deserted. I guess all the Moroccans were at work or doing housework. It wasn't a pretty beach, with plastic bottles and other refuse making it rather unattractive, so there was only the odd tourist. But there was the Atlantic. After a week crossing the desert and then more days on the bus I longed to get into the waves and submerge. "I'm going in in my underwear." "Not fair," said Maria. "I can't possibly go in in my bra and knickers. I'd be arrested." "Bad luck," I said. "You chose the wrong sex. Much better being a man." "I'm off, for a walk along the sand and a paddle. If you start to drown, don't shout for me. I'm not interested in saving a *man*!"

I dashed into the waves. I felt terrific. I couldn't stop swimming and diving. Eventually I saw Maria, waving to me to come in. I swam in. "Lunch time! Run around and get dry and then we will walk to a very local place along the beach."

I felt guilty. I was having fun on the beach with a woman while the other woman in my life was probably enslaved. I kept my thoughts to myself.

We had some fish right out of the sea, a beer and made a plan for the next morning. "We won't drive close. I want to catch this woman well before she gets to the house. In fact, you drop me off even further back. And turn the car round in case we have to make a quick getaway."

The sun shone and shimmered across a quiet sea. It was a cloudless, light blue, sky. It was excruciatingly hot. Only the fisherman around our beach café seemed to move, fiddling with their boats and their nets, preparing for tomorrow's early morning sea-safari. I didn't envy them. I know fishing for one fish is fun. Fishing for thousands is back-breaking work, and often dangerous if the weather suddenly breaks.

We talked about our lives. Where we had been raised. What we had studied. What our parents did and how we ended up being journalists. Maria was the daughter of a quite well-known novelist and her mother was a doctor. She pulled out a photo of her parents from her wallet. They were a handsome couple. I could see where Maria got her fine features from, her short nose, her straight black hair, her olive skin and the same brilliant smile as her mother. It was her father who encouraged her to go into journalism. He told her that since she had his writer's blood in her veins that was a good way to start. She'd had a happy childhood, she said. Her parents always stimulated her. Effortlessly, she realized now, she had absorbed their love of art, literature and ballet. Holidays were usually spent walking in the mountains, camping out wild, away from everybody. She missed them terribly. Three years ago they'd been killed in a car accident. I took her hand for a moment. She was softly crying. I beckoned the waiter and with a quiet nod ordered another two beers. Then Maria decided to tell me she had a husband. They'd been together since university. He was a dentist. She grimaced. "He's really not that interesting. It's just teeth and gums, teeth and gums. He's very good looking and charming and he supported me when my parents died but it's very up and down. Maybe if we had children it would be more fulfilling. One good thing is that he earns a lot and can subsidise expensive trips like this one." (I learnt later, after I had been a journalist for a few years, that there was a big problem for male free-lancers working abroad in faraway places because there were a lot of educated women out there—wives of diplomats, aid workers, lawyers, professors, businessmen and doctors—who, as kept women, were happy to work for a quite modest remuneration. They weren't particularly demanding on expenses. This was irresistible to cash-strapped editors. Why pay more for a man, even if the women were less experienced?)

I asked her what motivated her in life? "My grandfather's generation nearly destroyed Spain with the civil war. He was against Franco but I know his side just like the fascists committed unspeakable crimes. People of my generation don't talk about it much but I don't think we can walk away from our history quite so fast. I've pushed my father and grandfather to tell me all they know. Like Hanna Arendt I want to know how human beings can become so evil. I think by the time I was sixteen I was sure I wanted to spend my life exposing evil. Becoming a journalist was an obvious step. I've enjoyed the last six years so much. Before this story

I cracked one on Catholic nuns abusing children in their orphanage in Barcelona. I feel a bit guilty when I said "enjoy" just now. Ideally, I should dress in sackcloth but look at me now. A Georgio Armani blouse. One way and another I have a good income and I can do good. Is that a bad combination? Sometimes I get confused with myself. It's no use talking about these things to my dentist." I could see we were on the same wavelength.

Maria changed tack. "This afternoon, I'll take you to the old town and the souk. It's not as interesting as the capital, Rabat, and certainly not at all like Marrakesh. You must go there someday. It's one of the most fascinating places I have ever been to. In some ways it hasn't changed in 300 years."

Later, after a long walk along the seemingly endless beach, tired, dusty and sweaty, we made it back to the hotel. It was so hot that I surmised that even the flies had dozed off. We decided to swim in the pool. Maria, deprived this morning, couldn't wait. Then it was dinner, more chat, mainly about the changes triggered by the Arab Spring. In Morocco it had left a rather benign mark. Finally, an exhausted sleep and a wake-up call for six. I could see that our romantic days — or single night—were over. Now it was going to be slog and grind, blood, sweat and probably tears—and dangerous too.

In the first light of day we drove at a steady pace to the smugglers' house. A couple of hundred metres before the house Maria told me to stop and she jumped out. For a few seconds I watched her saunter up the street. As agreed, I turned the car round and opened the front doors. Facing that way we could make a quicker getaway if Maria had to run back. I got out and opened the bonnet and pretended to tinker with the engine, all the time looking at Maria who was barely moving, on the lookout for the maid.

Fifteen minutes or so later a motorbike pulled up at the house and a woman dismounted. The bike drove away. Maria had increased her pace and then tripped and fell. She let out a loud cry. This was all part of her plan. As expected, the woman heard her and turned. Maria sat up and cried again. The woman turned back and offered Maria her hand to pull her up. Maria told me later that the woman asked her where she was going. She told her that she liked to take a fast early morning walk, going in different directions. In fact, she was now a bit lost. The woman gave her directions. At that moment Maria pretended to faint. The woman's French was broken but they managed to communicate. "Come," she said, pointing, "I'll get you water."

They walked slowly to the house and Maria was able to take in the geography, the position of the windows, the size of the garden and notice where the guard stood. It was a typical house of the upper middle class. Constructed with uninspiring concrete — the "modern" building material, it was plainly painted in white to resist the near permanent glare of the sun. The guard was drinking a coffee and, judging from the litter of fag-ends, smoking probably his twentieth cigarette of the night while he waited to go off duty. The woman stopped to chat and presumably explained Maria's accident. I could tell from his gestures that he seemed reticent about letting Maria go further. The woman, I surmised, told Maria to wait there while she fetched her a glass of water. I saw Maria casually edging away from the guard so that when the woman reappeared they could chat without being overheard.

I was surprised how much information Maria gleaned in a short five minutes of low-key conversation. Apparently seven men lived in the house including the two guards. The maid rarely saw them go out during daylight and assumed from odd snatches of conversation she overheard that they liked to go out for a drive in the evening. Maria wandered how they could have girls hidden away in the house, until she noticed another, smaller house, tucked away off at the side surrounded and almost hidden by eucalyptus trees. Maria asked the woman who lived there. The woman explained she wasn't allowed there. One thing she thought odd—Maria had asked her if she liked to cook for so many—"I cook for twenty ... They sleep half the day. I ask where food goes. The man angry. Me quiet now. No want lose job. Good money."

Maria walked down to me and we drove off. Sitting in a quiet, café, shaded by red flame trees, back from the road, we dissected Maria's conversation. It was obvious that the small house contained the young women and girls. We knew where they were going. But where did they come from? Presumably they arrived after nightfall, so the maid never saw them, nor the neighbours.

Maria reasoned that the men had perhaps paid off the staff of an orphanage. Or they simply kidnapped girls on the quieter streets. Perhaps she suggested, as she thought aloud, they visited the brothels around town and pointed their guns at the pimp or the Madame. "Anyone can set up a small brothel in Casablanca, you don't have to be part of a gang," explained Maria. "There are a lot of free-lance pimps running small brothels with only half a dozen prostitutes. They daren't go to the police if a girl is kidnapped."

"So what next?" I couldn't see the steps ahead. "The police, you've said, can be bought off." "Not always" she replied. "But I have to find someone senior. If I explain to him that I'm a journalist for El País and that for big stories we link up with Le Monde, The Guardian, The New York Times and The International Herald Tribune I will probably get him to be cooperative."

"I'm going to go to our embassy and get some advice on who to talk to in the police. I'm going to phone a diplomat there I have been given an introduction to." She pulled out her phone and pressed the digits. In minutes she had an appointment for this afternoon.

She met up with the diplomat, and he had on his desk the name, private phone number and e-mail of a police superintendent who dealt with the drug trade who the embassy had a good reciprocal relationship with. He dialled. The policeman spoke Spanish. He suggested she come to his office.

She didn't invite me to join her. She said she felt I had nothing to contribute at this stage. Probably too she knew that a lone, attractive woman without a wedding ring—she had taken hers off—could make more progress than we together. I was left to my own devices. The girl at the hotel desk gave me directions to the English-language bookshop and I had a quiet hour seeing what they'd got. I returned to the hotel's swimming pool with half a dozen paperbacks including a couple of Ngũgĩ wa Thiong'o's novels, the Kenyan writer with an international reputation, and another two Ben Okris. I also bought a couple of translated Moroccan novels.

The hours passed and there was no sign of Maria. I had a drink and eventually dinner. At 11 there was still no sign of her, no phone call. Nothing. Why is it, I wondered, the women I work with just disappear? I didn't have the policeman's phone number or even the name of the diplomat. I went up to her room and knocked loudly. No answer. I returned to the lobby and asked if she had taken her key. No, she hadn't. I climbed into to bed full of anxiety. I tossed and turned for a long time before sleep took over. I woke up early and again I knocked on her door and downstairs checked if she had taken her key. She still hadn't. After a quick breakfast — just a coffee and croissant — I hired a cab to the Spanish embassy. I was going to wait at the gate and wait for the diplomat Maria knew to arrive at work. Half an hour later the staff trickled in. I went up to a woman and asked if she knew the diplomats. "There are only four," she said. "Of course, I know them all. I'm a secretary." I quickly explained the situation. She took me into the building and before long after she'd made a couple of phone calls I was sitting in the office of Maria's contact, a cheerful, bearded man, in his forties wearing an open shirt and a white linen jacket.

I told him that Maria had disappeared off my radar. He phoned the police superintendent who said he was just about to call him.

Maria had been to see him. He'd arranged for her to come back and meet him at nine and then the two of them plus a couple of constables would go down to the dock Maria had taken us too and take a look. She hadn't appeared at their rendezvous. The diplomat told him that I was here and was sure she'd not returned to the hotel.

Maria had gone AWOL and what the hell to do? The diplomat and I turned over the possibilities as we drove over to the superintendent's office. Our minds were blank. "Let's hope Ishmael has some ideas," he said. "Fuck. I'm worried." "Yes, fuck," I added. "I fear the worst, but that's stupid of me."

At the desk we told them our business and within moments we were whisked into Ishmael's enormous office—a big desk and a long conference table. Ishmael was small by our European standards, but muscular, nearly bald, around 50 and a non-stop smoker with a hacking cough. We sat down and he spread his hands. "This is a hard one." He looked at me and told me to tell him the full story from A to Z. I spent a good 20 minutes giving him every detail. Roberto, the diplomat, looked increasingly worried. Ishmael was a study in calmness.

After I finished the room fell silent. Ishmael didn't move. He seemed to be staring at the far wall. He lit another cigarette, pushed back his chair and began to pace the room. He didn't ask me any questions. "I think she was noticed when she talked to the maid. Maybe someone upstairs in the house looked out of the window and saw them talking. After all she was quite near the gate and obviously not the kind of person who would casually have a conversation with a maid. I think after she got back in the car you were followed. Followed to the hotel where she dropped you off, then the embassy and then to me. They waited for her to leave the police station and then someone abducted her as she walked back to your hotel. I take a guess — she's locked up with the young women in that house you speak of. I wouldn't be surprised if they have interrogated her, even a bit of light torturing. OK, she's 29, perhaps a bit old to be wanted in a Rio de Janeiro brothel but the traffickers might decide to give it a try. They want her out of Morocco and far away from the scene. They'll threaten her with acid on the face if she talks in Rio or wherever they take her. Last night you can be sure they moved the girls from that house and took them to another safe house. These wealthy, well-organised gangs have a number of those. Then they'll probably try and ship her out tonight since they will guess the police are probably alerted, as we are. The question is, was Maria brave enough to hide what she knew about the docks and the dark-windowed vans. Well, there is only one way to find out. This evening we will watch that gate you and Maria found. We won't lose anything. If Maria did confess they won't appear anywhere near the docks. They could even kill her. They might have a Plan B. They'll lie low for a week or more and then try and find another way to ship the girls out—maybe a small motorboat that makes a rendezvous with a big ship well off-shore. But let's do a check tonight."

I wandered back to the hotel in a daze. It was if the streets were empty. I'd lost two women in a matter of days. Ishmael had said he'd pick me up at eleven. The first thing I did at the hotel was to pull out my iPad and get up to date with the news. First, I read the BBC website, then the Guardian's and the Herald Tribune's which, on its front page had a headline: "26 young women from Africa found dead in the Mediterranean Sea." I read the report, "The bodies were taken to Spain where officials said they were investigating how the women died. 'It is a tragedy for mankind', said Antonio Chavez, the prefect in the port city of Cadiz where the bodies arrived with 400 other migrants who were rescued in recent days."

"The young women were estimated to be between the ages of 14 and 18." Marco Rotunno, the communications officer for the UN High Commission for Refugees, commented that "when such groups of young women and girls are alone, the probability is high that they are victims of sex trafficking rings."

I took my time eating dinner. I drank only one glass of wine, determined to have all my wits about me.

At eleven on the dot Ishmael and his bodyguard of two arrived. We drove down to the docks while Ismail explained his plan. They had on their uniforms and gun belts, and he was simply going to intimidate the guards on the gate. The two policemen also carried rifles. He parked the car some distance away and then strode up to the gate. Three minutes later he beckoned us to come. We went through the gate and one of the guards walked us to near the suspected ship. It was stacked with crates and containers. We hid in one of the narrow corridors between two rows of crates. The now familiar gloom shaded our faces.

About two hours later we heard a van draw up on the dock. Then the light padding of many female feet. We looked through the dark and we could see for a brief second two men at the back of the file, carrying torches. Minutes later we heard the clanging of the bolts being drawn back on the door of a container. Then we heard the shrieks of the women and girls as they were herded in. The bolts were shoved in. Suddenly there was silence. A minute later we heard the three men's footsteps.

Ishmael crept forward as the men got into the van. He'd already told the guard on the gate to take their registration number and look at the colour of the van. In moments the van had disappeared.

Ishmael called the station and gave the registration number to a colleague. "We will have no trouble picking them up," he said. He also asked for a car to be sent down with tools for breaking a lock. Within twenty minutes the women and girls were free. And there was Maria, looking a bit the worse for wear but rushing towards me, giving me the longest hug I'd ever been given.

Ishmael dropped us off at the hotel and told us to come to his office at noon the next day. He had already booked rooms for the girls in a pension.

"Time to celebrate," said Maria. "I'm free and I've got the story, so it's champagne—as many bottles as we can drink! She told me what had happened and the surmises of Ishmael were exactly right.

We almost rolled down our corridor. I was about to hug her goodnight when she took my hand and whispered, "I've got a present for you. I owe you my life." She unlocked her door and we went in. She pulled at my shirt and lifted it over my head.

Half an hour later we made love again and then fell asleep in each other's arms. We slept until eleven. Maria had woken a few minutes before me and had put on the room's kettle. We drank our coffee, luxuriating in each other's company. "That was amazing. The whole thing. What a story I've got. As for our time in bed I'm shattered with good feelings. I know I said it last time, but there will be no more sex. After last time I felt guilty about my husband. This time I didn't. But if there is a third and a fourth time I'll be riddled with bad, bad feelings. Right, let's shower, grab another croissant and get a taxi to the office. Move fast, my dearest Jon. Otherwise we'll be late." She shoved me in the direction of the shower. I hadn't had a moment to get a word in edgeways.

The taxi crawled through the traffic. "Let's get out and walk," I suggested. "Or we'll never get there in time." Ishmael was waiting for us. "It didn't take us long to trace the van and then the house. We've arrested six of them. They are now in the cells here in the basement awaiting trial. There were another dozen girls in a shed who had obviously arrived yesterday. A fast turnover business! They are in the same pension as the others. I'll have to work out how we send them home. I've got a female officer at the pension right now interviewing them."

"I have a question," I said. I told him the story about Agnes and me and our quest. I have to say this busy man was exceedingly patient and heard me out for a good half hour. I told him about the deal Maria and I had. I was helping her and she would help me.

"Well, I see you two are skilled sleuths," he said smiling. "How can I help you?" "Just give us advice in which city or town or village you think Agnes might be in." "That's a hard one. We are talking about a vast distance, three different countries and more than three separate police forces." He lit a cigarette and ordered us coffee. Finally, he spoke. "Not in Morocco. Too far for the traffickers to travel — and unnecessary too. As you know there's a good market for slaves in Mauritania. They're not exporting girls and young women as they do here. They're not so sophisticated. My guess is that they would sell them in Nouakchott. There are many rich families there and the husbands can take concubines without any social disgrace. I'll give you the phone number of the police chief there. He's an amiable and I think fairly competent guy. I met him at a conference of West African police chiefs a couple of years ago. Of course, he might be corrupt. I've no way of telling."

We thanked Ishmael profusely. I could see Maria shocked him a bit by putting her arm around his neck and giving him a peck on the cheek.

As we walked back to the hotel we tried to formulate a plan. "We'll hire a four-wheel drive," Maria said. "I don't like the idea of those night-time buses you told me about and I know my editor will pay me expenses now I've got him this story — and perhaps I'll get him another. We don't have to rush like crazy people. Some night stops and sleepovers will keep us fit and sharp."

"Right, now I'm going to write my story and file it. I'm skipping lunch. See you for dinner. I'll find you at the swimming pool."

Around six Maria found me at the pool. "I've done it and sent it off," she shouted, smiling. And with that she dived into the pool. She did a fast crawl, much faster than anything I can do with my breaststroke, the only style I've mastered.

I day-dreamed — who was the prettiest of my two women? Maria, who I can never win, comes out on top of my league table. But where do these thoughts get me? A bit superficial, maybe, although one can't ignore it. Physical chemistry is a big, big thing in a human being's life. Both of them have given me the shakes. But I'm aware enough, even at my youthful age, to know falling in love with the right person for me is about character. As that clever and perceptive Nigerian woman writer, Chimamanda Ngozi Adiche, has written, "You don't fall in love, you climb up to love."

They both are empathetic women, feeling strongly about how to ameliorate the downtrodden, the poorest, those at the bottom of the barrel. If it's about imagination, if it's about brain power, I think they are both very bright. I guess it's about culture too. Maria comes from my background and has told me she loves classical music including ballet and opera, theatre, film and novels. But then too she says she often prefers popular history novels with a heavy romantic ingredient—not my taste at all. And she is not as earnest as me about reading. I devour books—a bookaholic, as one friend said. Give me a classic or this year's Booker Prize short list, politics, a history, a travel book, and something on the media, economics and science, as long as they are not written in academic jargon, and I'll devour them. Academics should copy the ease of access to profound ideas that Stephen Hawking did so well. Maria is not like me in all aspects, I conclude, although I admire her very much. With Agnes I can't remember when she talked about a novel unless I brought it up. I've no idea what Agnes likes and dislikes apart from South African and Tanzanian music. I'm always surprised that when I meet a bright and well-educated African often they know little about African books, apart from the Nobel Prize winner for literature, Wole Soyinka.

My daydreaming came to a sudden stop before I could finish my thoughts. Maria was throwing handfuls of water on my hot, sun-drenched, body. "How about a cocktail by the pool?" she laughed, shaking the water from her long black hair all over me. "I'll get them." I groaned to myself. "Lucky husband, does the dentist who never leaves his drill alone know it?" She turned tail before I lifted myself up.

She returned with two Italian-type Camparis, now my favourite drink apart from red wine. "I've been thinking while swimming. The more I wrote of my article on the sex trade the more I realized what a scoop we've got. I wouldn't be surprised if we win a prize for it. Then I'll see you again at the awards ceremony. You see, you will never escape my grasp!" "Don't tease me like that," I said, smiling a big grin. I fired back: "After we find Agnes, I don't want to see you ever again. You are a bad woman. You make love to me and leave me." Maria let out a great big belly laugh and stroked my hair. "Well, if you hadn't been a bad boy you wouldn't be in such an emotional tangle. I don't feel sorry for you. You didn't have to kiss me." We went back and forth. "Now I've got the measure of your character," I said, "I'm not so sure that you are as innocent as you make yourself out to be. How many times have you been unfaithful?" "Actually, you are the only one and I hope you are the last. Inside I feel very disturbed."

"Enough serious talk about romantic twaddle," I interjected, a little crossly. Didn't she know she had left *me* rather disturbed? "Where are we going to eat?" "I know another, simple, local place, classic local food and clean," Maria suggested. "Let's go and get dressed."

We met in the lobby and walked out into the warm evening air. "I'm going to take you on a bit of a detour," Maria said. "Before we leave you just have to see the spectacular grand mosque. It stands near the edge of a cliff and faces out over the sea." We walked fast for twenty minutes and came to the sea. It was indeed fantastic. "Most of the Arabs who invaded Spain in the 9th century were Moors who came from Morocco," Maria explained as we wandered around inside, amazed by its bold strength but simplicity of its architecture. The main prayer room was massive. Enormous crystal chandeliers hung from the high ceiling. "The Moors joined forces with other Arabs coming from the Middle East.

Sometimes when Maria gets going she's hard to stop. It was all fascinating but I was getting peckish. I gently edged her out of the mosque. The sea was glowing very slightly, gradually darkening into blackness as we looked towards the horizon, yet retaining here and there a skin of almost phosphorescent light, but uninviting, even ominous. High above us were the clear, almost translucent, stars. "I don't believe in God," said Maria, looking up and then pausing, seeming to count the vast firmament of silver dots. Then she inhaled sharply and continued her thought. "Perhaps I should have fallen on my knees inside the mosque to thank him for giving me life and it not being taken away here in Morocco." She was quiet for a minute. "Let's hurry. I'm hungry."

Early the next morning we left Casablanca behind us, heading south. Compared with my northward journey this was paradise — a luxurious model of a hired Land Rover, complete with air-conditioning, bottles of water and beer kept cold in a special clay pot filled with ice. Then there was Maria's Spanish touch — chorizo, cheese, olives, carrots and oranges. Maria had packed her CDs. She decided she'd drive the first leg. I was happy to be left to sort through them and put them in the order I wanted to play them — Mozart string quartets to start with, Chopin's preludes next, and then some Paul McCartney.

This time we had a map of the West African coast I'd bought in the English bookshop. On the net I'd found a list of towns that claimed they had hotel accommodation. There were a few, but not many, entries on TravelSite written by hard-bitten travellers. "Reading this, I'm not sure the accommodation will suit my Spanish princess," I joked as we cruised at a comfortable 100 km an hour. "Find a place that doesn't have bed bugs," said Maria, "Anything else I can cope with."

A bit to my surprise, in mid-afternoon we made it through the Moroccan frontier post in a matter of minutes. Now we were in Western Sahara, so utterly poor, down-at-heel and desolate compared with Morocco. I knew we were unlikely to get to the Mauritanian border until after dark. We had already decided not to drive at night. We didn't want to hit a large animal at speed or be waylaid by some wild young guerrilla soldiers, mistaking us for Moroccan secret agents.

I had my mind on a small fishing town, marked on the map as Asoo. To my surprise I'd seen there were three small hotels listed. I suppose the fishing trade brought in buyers. "Maria — do you mind our sheets smelling of day-old fish?" "No, I don't mind if it stops you tempting me." She grabbed my hair, making me swerve.

The hours peeled away. There wasn't much to look at. Once you've seen one lot of desert scrubland you have seen it all. Occasionally we passed through small villages, usually with a rundown shop or two selling Coca-Cola and mobile phone cards, and out in the country Bedouin boys shepherding their fathers' goats. We stopped at one of the villages and Maria phoned one of the hotels. From time to time we saw signs pointing to phosphate mines. But even with the mines nearby the traffic was thin—maybe half a dozen trucks and another half dozen cars every hour. Occasionally they threw up dust right in front of us. There was no tarmac. We closed the windows and Maria would slow down.

The sunset was in full colour when we saw the outline of the town we were aiming for. We turned off the main road towards the ocean. On our right, to the north, we could see bright orange clouds like the robes of Tibetan monks. Far out to sea to the northwest we could see dark black rain clouds. And to the southwest, pointing towards Brazil, sharp yellow clouds. I thought of a hundred pretty Marias, dressed as buttercups, about to prance across this illuminated grand stage in some great production of Midsummer Night's Dream danced by the Rio ballet.

"Good timing," I said. "Are you a good lay?" she grinned. "I mean will you lie all night on the bed bugs and I'll sleep on top of you?" Maria's colloquial English was spot on. I was full of joy, like the song of a violin.

As it turned out it was quite a decent little hotel. Only six rooms, clean toilet and bathroom and with white, sun-bleached, sheets. The landlord told us the restaurant would be open in an hour.

The landlord must have assumed we were married and gave us one room. When we realized we'd only been given one key I asked the landlord why, making myself look a bit stupid. I looked at Maria and she just smiled. "You, see when I phoned him I said I was on my honeymoon trip!" "The hell you did," I interjected. She bent over and laughed and couldn't stop. Even the landlord was amused, not that he could understand one word. "Come on, let's have a shower." I'm shedding my inhibitions, so get moving if you want it!"

I was stunned. I sat on the bed while she showered. I'd tried to convince myself, obviously unsuccessfully, that I wanted nothing more than her smile and her affection. Is a growingly intense sexual relationship what I truly wanted? Could I stop myself? If we carried on like this where did it end? If we found Agnes what would she feel when she saw that we were sleeping together? When we went back to Tanzania how could I bear to say goodbye to Maria who would return in the opposite direction to live as the loyal wife of a Madrid dentist. Which woman did I want? Was my destiny being written by sex? Come on, I told myself. Maria was an exceptional journalist and a compassionate and empathetic human being, but ...

My thoughts were truncated. Maria walked out of the shower and came across the room and stood in front of me.

We had a good meal with very fresh white fish for dinner plus some OK Moroccan wine. Weary after so many hours of driving we headed upstairs for an early night. We just had to make love one more time before sleep took over.

The next day I took the driver's seat. The sun was partly behind us as we drove, so that we seemed to be in pursuit of our own shadows. My thoughts nagged at me. The texture of life was all heaviness, nastiness, worry and sometimes fear. I didn't know if we would find Agnes and I didn't know how I would deal with the situation if we did. One of the qualities—if that is the word—of a bad time is that it seems endless.

By late evening, we were in Nouakchott. We checked in at the hotel I had stayed in before. We were rather buzzed after two whole days on the road and the streetlights were dim. Nevertheless, we strolled around, looked in the shops and read the posters outside the cinema. We found a bar but then realized that life in Mauritania was of the strict variety. Only in "Western" hotels could alcohol be found. We downed our fresh orange juice and pretended to race each other to the bar in the hotel.

We were so dried out and dehydrated after the journey we both switched to beer. I drank two, one after the other, and then began to feel normal. I think it was the same for Maria. It took us a while to talk and then when we did there wasn't much to say. We had talked ourselves out, cooped up as we had been in the Land Rover. We had already made a rough plan for tomorrow, starting with the Spanish embassy, then with the American one and then with the police chief, and going on from there. "There" about summed it up. We hadn't much of a clue.

We did our usual thing: a loll in the hotel's very nice, palm-lined, swimming pool and then dinner on the terrace. "Tomorrow is another day," I whispered to Maria, as I switched the light out.

We were at the Spanish embassy at nine. Maria, using her Madrid contacts, had got us an interview with the ambassador, who turned out be rather young—35ish to 40—I would guess—for such a senior post. She said immediately, "just call me Ana." I assume her superiors in Madrid thought that if she could hack it here then such a sharp woman could be promoted quickly.

Maria started to tell our whole story, in Spanish. She told me to switch off and relax, that it was quicker this way. She talked non-stop. All I could do was look at the intelligent eyes of the ambassador and how she would furry her brow or hold up hands, presumably in horror. Finally, she intervened in English. "Look, my friends, I've got quite a bit on this morning. But at two the embassy closes. It's too hot to work, say the Mauritanians, so we work until 2 without any lunch. Then I'll meet you at this place." She scribbled a note.

We ordered lunch—couscous with lamb—and three cold beers. Even under the restaurant's awning it was almost too hot to talk. "Maybe we should take our lunch to the car and turn the air conditioning on" I suggested. Maria started to talk, presumably thinking there had been too much to digest in the story in one sitting.

After a minute, Ana said, "That's OK. I remember it all from this morning," switching to almost perfect English. "Let's concentrate on what to do. Frankly this is not my scene. Madrid does worry about migration, but we don't have the same problems as some other European countries. We need labour, especially when the oranges are ripe and the vines are ready to be plucked. The Spanish people appreciate that. Then we are very fortunate. We are one of the three countries in Europe that doesn't have a truly significant racist party, Well, with Vox, the extreme right wing party, their big things are devolution and women's rights, not so much immigration. " "Yes, I've read about that," I interjected. "The other two are Portugal and Luxembourg."

"In the EU we push for more development funds and expertise," continued Ana. "With more development at this end people wouldn't feel the urge to migrate. From what I've heard Mauritania could do well if some of the genetically improved crops, good in dry soils, were introduced here. But the government is corrupt and concentrates its efforts, such as they are, on urban voters.

"As for the EU, it is only just getting round to dealing with development issues. You 20– and 30-year-olds– may not believe it but there were newspaper and academic articles about this growing migration issue and sometimes with good ideas about what to do about it back when I was at university but politicians and governments don't seem able to read or think beyond the end of their noses." She sighed. "But, as I said, I'm no expert. I'm an economist and I concentrate on exports and banking. There's a lot of money-laundering here that I'm supposed to gather evidence on. But I do try and keep up with my reading. There's not much else to do here after work.

"One thing I do know is that a great opportunity has been missed. My previous posting was to South Korea. In the 1950s it was as poor as Africa today. Then there was a civil war and much of the country was decimated. But look at South Korea today. Land reform got the whole thing going. Before, serfdom held most people back. In fact, the Japanese occupiers during the Second World War did a useful thing. They implemented the kind of land reform that had been introduced at home during the Meiji Restoration. That was how and why modern Japan took off and that's how, later, South Korea got going."

We both were stimulated by the ambassador who seemed to be a non-stop talker, but it wasn't really what we had come to see her about. Maria gently led the conversation back to Agnes. "Do you have any ideas on where we should start?"

"Maybe with the American ambassador. It's quite a big and sophisticated embassy. The Americans have a state-of-the-art listening post here. They track Russian submarines in the Atlantic and keep a watch on the African fishing boats which they think are used as transport for imported Latin American drugs. Then there is the piracy that began in recent years, emulating the piracy on the eastern side of Africa, particularly off the Somali coast. They have some fast boats and, with the approval of the government, venture out to sea to intercept suspected ships. Their clever modern radar systems and listening receivers do a great job, I'm told.

"I know the ambassador. On early Saturday mornings before it gets hot I play tennis with him and a few others. He knows a lot and he's not too bureaucratic. Maybe he could use his formidable search machines to do some tracking on land. Let's see if I can get an appointment for the three of us."

At eleven the next morning we sat in the ambassador's office. Coffee was served and we had some small chit-chat about the drive down from Morocco which he had never done. "Now tell me, what brings you here. Ana, you start."

"First, I must say one thing. This concerns a Tanzanian journalist, a colleague of Jon, who has disappeared while on assignment. There is no Tanzanian embassy here so I've got authority from Madrid to take her under my wing."

Maria and I took turns to tell our story so far. He was attentive. "You know it's a hard nut to crack and there are many vested interests. The government is ambivalent. We do what we can do. After all it gets a lot of money from us. We pay a sizeable rent for our monitoring station. They know if they resist us on too many things we'll up stakes and move to Morocco or Senegal. So how do you think I can help you? I would say one thing before you speak—this police chief who you have an introduction to is a first-class investigator. He may be a bit corrupt, but he is useful, very useful, to have as an ally. Not much goes on in the city that he doesn't know about."

Ana spoke. "You have all this sophisticated intelligence equipment and presumably you have agents on the ground, and you know the police chief. Could you somehow arrange for them to look for Agnes?"

He hadn't been expecting this question. He put his fingers together and was quiet. Then came his answer. "I guess, I could, but only for a week and that must be part time, otherwise I'll get a rocket from Washington."

"Terrific, that's great," the three of us all said at once. Ana got straight to the point. "How will this be done?" He pressed a buzzer on his desk and a secretary appeared. "See if Bill Rogers is in the building. If not get him on the phone. Bill is my intelligence chief. He's like Obama, the son of a mixed marriage, and he has a colour that lets him blend in."

He called the police chief. Obviously, he was fluent in English. The ambassador gave a summary of the situation and asked if he would meet us. That was fixed for early evening. The secretary walked back in. "I found Bill. He's coming right up."

The ambassador asked her to bring some more coffee. Bill walked in and sat down. I could see he had an easy relationship with the ambassador. "Gosh," said Ana. "You're in our tennis group. You said you were the Coca-Cola representative. Now I see that was just a cover story!" He smiled.

The ambassador gave him a quick summary. We filled in some of the bits and pieces.

"What can you do for them, Bill? Bill put his head down and seemed to be looking at the pattern on the carpet. Then he said, "If only our technology could send a signal into every rich person's house we would track her down fast — you have convinced me that is where she is most likely to be. No, it's got to be hard slog by our agents. By the way, many of them are local, speaking the language. If the police chief is charmed by you this evening then he can deploy a lot of help too. Jon, stay back in the hotel. You can re-enter the picture tomorrow. This guy loves women! Ladies, if he asks you out to dinner, accept. He won't harm you. Of course, we will coordinate with him."

We wandered around the town all afternoon. Ana had gone back to her house for a siesta after having volunteered to Maria that she would come to dinner this evening. Maria, I could see, was much relieved.

The town centre, as I'd seen before, was of modest size. We got the hang of it in a thirty-minute walk. All of the buildings seemed to be built of the same dull concrete. In front of some of them there had been a desultory attempt to nurture some plant life but it was obvious that it was a bit of a useless struggle. The noxious mixture of sea air, lack of rain and a beating sun made for a cruel environment when it came to vegetation. The city seemed to sag. Perhaps it would come apart at the seams.

We launched ourselves down a side road. For the next kilometre we walked past large houses, all set back from the road with high walls with barbed wire at the top. Every house had an armed guard at the gate, standing solitary, under an umbrella to keep off the burning sun. Occasionally we saw a car going in or coming out of a house. Invariably they were Mercedes. There weren't many people on the road and those that we saw looked more like cooks and gardeners than wealthy owners.

After a tiring walk we looped back. We tried a road on the opposite side of the town square. It was the same.

We were both worn out and hadn't had much to say to each other as we fought the sun. "Let's take a break," I said. "How about a cool fresh fruit juice?" We headed to a café. "No fresh juices, only canned," the waiter said. "How come?" we both asked. "Have you seen any fruit trees growing?" replied the waiter. "Look at our weather. Down by the sea we have coconut palms, but that's it."

Maria said, "Let's go, I saw a boy selling coconuts on the corner. We can drink the milk. It's refreshing, cool and very nutritious." We bought a couple and sat under a tree on a bench in a little park in the centre of the square, both of us just staring into the distance, drinking the coconut milk and wishing the torpid heat would evaporate, disappear or sink into the sea.

"I need to be air-conditioned," Maria's gentle voice awoke me from my reverie. "Let's go to the hotel, have lunch, then a swim and work out what we should do this afternoon."

It turned out to be air-conditioning, sex, swim, lunch and thinking, in that order. We agreed that we should see the rest of the city — the poorer parts, even though there would be little chance Agnes would be there.

We took a taxi a couple of kilometres. In five minutes we were well inside the shanty town, outside a little shop. We paid the driver off and asked him to meet us there in two hours' time.

I'd seen a lot of locals walking around with umbrellas to ward off the sun. I ducked through the shop's low doorway and to my delight saw a pile of umbrellas.

Thus armed we set off for a stroll. I just wanted to get the lay of the land. Maria, more experienced than me, said we have to find someone who speaks English who we could pay to be our interpreter. That wasn't so easy though there was a café, bar or shop on every street corner, even a couple of hairdressers and a shop selling phone cards and cheap, early model, mobile phones. There were no overhead wires, Maria pointed out, so no electricity. Later we discovered that the phone shops had generators to re-charge their customers' phones. God knows what the government spent its revenue on from the phosphate mines. The houses were built mainly of mud with corrugated iron roofs.

After our fourth stop we struck lucky. We had gone from customer to customer asking who spoke English. There was a young man, downing a beer in a small bar, who had worked as a foreman in one of the American-owned mines where he had had to learn English to liaise between the workers and the American supervisors. We bought him another beer and two for ourselves and told him why we wanted help. He explained he lived at the mine but was back home for a week to visit his widowed mother. I could see he rather liked the idea of interpreting for us. We settled a rate. His name was Salim.

"Just show us around this place to get us started," said Maria. "Sure, Ok, Let's hit the road," he replied in an American drawl. We smiled at each other. Texas in the Sahara Desert.

Off the main street it was just alleyways. Down the side of the paths was a trench full of strips of newspaper and what looked like dried out turds. "Is there no sanitation?" I asked. He shook his head. "They either dry out or get washed away when it rains. But it only rains for a few days a year." "Where does your water come from?" "If you keep walking up the main street in 200 metres you will see a well. That's what we depend on." When will these poverty-stricken people be able to cleanse themselves from the squalor of the shanty town, I thought, and from the meanness of Mauritania's foreign exploiters and the indifference of the country's upper and middle class?

"Do you have a doctor nearby?" "No, but the municipality send a nurse round once a month, mainly to examine the pregnant women and to talk about birth control, but the women aren't very persuadable. I tried to get my 16-year-old cousin to see the nurse and she said to me, "What's the point of sex if you have a wrapper on the lollipop?" "Well, that's a new one," laughed Maria. "The sooner they start giving them pills and injections instead of condoms, the sooner the birth rate will go down." "Oh yeah," I interjected, "What about AIDS?" She shrugged.

We continued our conducted tour. To my surprise we came on a sign announcing a junior school. "How does that exist?" "The parents pay. They are desperate for their kids to be educated. You will find quite a few little schools in this neighbourhood."

We passed a shop with a sign announcing it was a pharmacist. We went in. With Salim's help I asked what medicines they had. It seemed it was limited to aspirins, Malaria prophylactics, cough medicine and antiseptic. "Do you sell many condoms?" I asked the woman. "From time to time," she replied, non-committedly.

"You know how the men relieve themselves?" Salim asked. "I'll tell you. They do it in plastic bags. Then when they've piled up 10 or so they walk or bike to the edge of the town and throw them on the wasteland. They call them 'flying toilets'."

Inwardly I gulped. I knew that diseases like smallpox, river blindness, polio and measles had all but been eliminated in Africa and that Malaria cases were falling steadily, as had the percentage of the poor, but to see this poverty first-hand underlined to me what I had long known, it was going to be a long battle. But not that long ago the average life span was around 40. These days it was nearer 60. There *is* progress.

"Maria, look at where we are and what we see. I can't imagine that these poor locals would be dealing in slaves." Salim overheard me. "Don't be so sure. Slaves can be bought for very little and the owners spend a pittance on keeping them. Look, there are people here who are small businessmen and have some money to spend. I'll walk you round. First, there are the cafes and bars. Look, there's a charcoal maker. He needs someone to go round with a bike selling the stuff. See that lorry. That's owned by a relatively wealthy man who probably earns his living by delivering stuff to the shops and bars and bringing in cement for people to build with. You will see a minibus before long, crammed with people coming back from work in the city. These sorts of things are quite profitable and maybe the owner's wife would like a slave in the kitchen."

We looked at each other. Where do we start? There were over half a million people living in the city's shanty towns. Maria was shaking her head. "I'm still pretty much convinced that a 'superior', well-educated slave like Agnes wouldn't be sold for a few dollars to these kind of people."

135

"We can't be sure," I said. "Whilst we have Salim let's poke around a bit." "Salim, where should we start?" "I think we should walk in the direction of my mother's house. The guys in the bars round there all know me and we may get some tips."

Ten minutes' walk away was a well-built, although smallish, house, whitewashed with a garden attached, growing vegetables. I could see tomatoes and bright yellow sun flowers whose seeds people use to extract their cooking oil. His grey-haired mother, a bit stooped, was in the garden, with a watering can. Salim introduced us and told his mother what he was up to and who we were. Close up the old mother looked haggard and was almost toothless. She smiled and welcomed us. "Do you remember your old teacher, Mahbub? He's retired but lives over there. He spends half the day in the bar, as far as I can tell. He seems to know everything. You should see the shelves of books in his house. He's a very special kind of man. He could have got a job in a better part of town, but he wanted to help the poor. After you have talked to him come back and have a cup of coffee."

We trooped over the road and met Mahbub as he was talking to a neighbour. A white-haired old man with his hair cut down almost to the crown of his head, he remembered Salim as soon as Salim explained when he had been at the school and who his mother was.

"My mother is making coffee for us. Please come." We wandered back to the house and found ourselves in a neat dining room with a simple table and half a dozen wooden chairs. Salim's mother brought in the coffee and a plate of biscuits.

Salim explained to the teacher the story of Agnes. "I know slavery goes on and there are probably some slaves here and there," Mahbub said, while fidgeting with what was left of his crinkled hair. "But I don't think it's a big problem in this neighbourhood. Besides it's not too hard to run away. The Imam in the mosque or the local priest would probably help you. They are the people where escaping slaves might turn to for help." "But Mohammed allowed slavery and Jesus and St Paul never condemned it," I interjected. "You are right, said the old man, but today most Muslims and Christians think it's wrong. I know my country has a bad reputation for slavery but I do believe most people are against it. I think you will find it practised mostly by the rich, but not by that many ordinary people."

"So how many people are we talking about," asked Ana. "How big is this corrupt class?" Mahbub fiddled with his hair, drank some coffee and was obviously thinking hard. "To tell you the truth. I've never thought about it in terms of numbers before. But I suppose it must be around three or four thousand. I might be wrong. It could be 500. It could be 5,000."

We decided to get back to town. The appointment with the police chief was in a couple of hours and we wanted to take a break from the heat before Maria went off for dinner with him and Ana.

The taxi was waiting for us outside the shop, parked under a mass of purple blossom, a jacaranda tree. I smiled to myself—I'd come a long way from Iringa's jacarandas. We told Salim we would be in touch soon. He had a mobile phone, and we took down the number.

At six Maria departed for the rendezvous. Ana was waiting and soon a rather small and undistinguished-looking man walked up to them and introduced himself, "I'm Sartaj Haq,"

Later, Maria gave me a summary of the evening's talk. Meanwhile, I was left in the hotel to amuse myself. I caught up on the news, wrote to my mother and father in Oxford and then went down to the restaurant with my novel. I really felt I'd dug myself into a hole as far as women were concerned. What was the adage? Oh yes, I remembered. "What's the First Law of Holes? When you get into a hole stop digging." I tried hard to put the women out of my mind. Two hours later Maria and Ana appeared. "A drink, please," panted Maria. "He took us to a place without alcohol. The food was delicious but do we need a drink!"

-

They sat down. I called over the waiter and then I got the story. "A really nice guy," said Ana. "Well educated, shrewd, and knowledgeable. He spoke good English. He'd done a masters in criminology at Columbia University in New York. He seems to know everyone important. While we were eating two cabinet ministers came up to him to say hello. It looked like it is the restaurant where la crème de la crème eats."

"I liked him," Maria said. "He had a great sense of humour and he confessed to us he had two wives and six children. He said he loved both wives equally." I interjected to tell them the story of my encounter with the chief in Senegal and his three wives. "I'd never slept with three women before," I joked. "Two was my record until this journey." Ana looked a bit taken aback. "Just kidding," I said. "Not true." The women laughed. "Get on with your story," I said. "If I do you will have to stop telling us your idiotic jokes," smiled Maria.

"We told him the whole story. Now I could recite it in my sleep," said Maria. "He listened without saying a word. When I was done he asked me lots of sharp questions." "She gave good answers—thoughtful ones, I thought," observed Ana. "I added the little I know."

"So what did he suggest?" I was in a hurry to get to the heart of the matter. "Well," Ana spoke slowly. "He thinks she could be here with a rich family or she could be with a relatively poor one, like in the neighbourhood we visited today of which there are many. The former is more likely but we shouldn't erase the possibility of the second."

I banged the table with my spoon. "Fuck this, we will never find her." "That's the bad news," said Ana grabbing my arm. "But the good news is that it is possible to move quite fast with police help. He says he's got the city covered with informers in every neighbourhood who for a regular stipend are his listening and watching posts. Anything unusual gets to his desk quite fast. He said that normally a slave girl wouldn't be noticed but one who looks educated, who comes from the other side of the continent, who tries to communicate in Swahili and English, would get talked about. Even in the richer neighbourhoods word would leak out through domestic staff. Tomorrow he's going to alert his informers."

"So you see," Maria observed, "We made progress. And then we have our American spy friend hard at work. We can do some checking on our own too, like we did this morning. Salim is a good interpreter."

I asked Ana why she thought the police chief was prepared to help us. "I can think of a couple of reasons. The Americans are important to this government and we've managed to get them interested — and, frankly, the police's local agents are a bit under-employed at the moment. The last three years the government has become more democratic and more stable, and there is less underground political activity going on. Crime is pretty low. Second, Spain is the country's biggest market for iron ore and phosphate and Agnes is now under my diplomatic wing."

"Phew," I said. "I never in my life thought I'd end up here with this problem. Maria, can you see if I have some grey hairs?" "Isn't this good for our characters?" Maria commented. "After this, if we find her, we'll feel we are ready for anything life can throw at us."

"And if we don't ... I think I'll go into a monastery to expiate my sins ... I've become a woman-let-downer."

"For God's sake, Jon," Maria interjected. "Don't be so maudlin. You are doing your best and if you have been a bit naughty in bed on the way, I don't think God minds too much. You haven't hurt anyone yet." She winked at Ana.

"Yet," I echoed. "Waiter, I need a double brandy. Anyone else?" Maria and Ana laughed. Ana got up to go. "Let's meet for dinner tomorrow evening and compare notes."

That night we didn't feel like sex. We fell into a deep sleep with our arms locked around each other.

I woke up first. I fired up my computer to take a look at the news. Nothing relevant. I then googled Mauritania to refresh my mind. The French had tried without success to abolish slavery here in 1905. The independent government had another go as recently as 1981. But only 10 years ago had the government passed a law saying that slave owners had to be prosecuted.

Despite this "flurry" of legislation Mauritania had the highest proportion of slaves of any country in the world. Black Africans had been captured since the days of the Europeans' slave trade — by light skinned Berbers or Berber-Arabs.

Trying not to disturb Maria I showered, dressed and went down in the cool of the early morning for breakfast. I grabbed both our swimsuits from the bathroom, ready for our morning swim. It had become a necessary part of our routine. I stepped out into the dense morning light.

Half an hour later she joined me. She looked very pretty. But every time I had such a thought I felt guilty. I wondered how she felt when she took her first look of the day at me.

"Eat well," I advised. "Goodness knows at what time we'll eat again. Let's look at the map and plan where to go. I suggest we phone Salim, arrange to pick him up and then go to the next neighbourhood and work our way through the city like that."

That's what we did. We were in Salim's capable hands and we let him do the deciding. He was throwing his energy into our quest almost as much as we were.

We made the phone call, took a swim and grabbed a taxi.

It was a tough day. We covered four neighbourhoods. In the first one Salim knew a couple of bars he occasionally dropped in on. They produced nothing, though in one case the landlord knew who in the surrounding streets had a slave — it was just a guy with a bus and the owner of the big bar 100 metres away, "They look like village girls, only speaking their tribal language, not educated."

I agreed with Salim's plan and off we went to the next and the next and the next. The heat was now extraordinary. Above 40°C. There was a gentle wind blowing in from the languid sea but it was strong enough to stir the dust and for the grit to get into our eyes. It was after 2 o'clock and we were very tired and hungry. We'd walked miles. "Eat and then siesta," ordered Maria. She popped into a bar and ordered a taxi.

Soon we were eating fish and some sort of green vegetable in a roadside cafe. We ate and I was getting more and more sleepy. The heat was a monster. "Now I know why you Spaniards like a siesta" "Let's go, said Maria. Do you want to make love or are you, old man, too dead, out of it?"

We emerged from our hotel at 4ish. We were meeting Ana at 6.30. "Ok, deep breath, one more neighbourhood." I phoned Salim. This time I gave him some money. He had never asked for an advance but he was obviously pleased.

The same routine. Bars, cafes, shops, the school, the Imam, and this time we found a church, Seventh-day Adventists. "I don't know if these guys have priests or ministers but there must be someone in charge, probably in that house next door." We knocked and a quite well-dressed middle-aged man opened the door. Without waiting for an explanation, he invited us in. It was cool inside and he offered us water. A youngish girl brought the glasses in. She was poorly dressed, in sharp contrast to the man. "Your daughter?" Maria asked. "Oh no, she's our sort-of servant. Actually, we bought her as a slave but that was because we wanted to set her free. She can't remember where she came from. She is traumatised. We are just giving her time to recover and for her memory to come back and then we'll try and find her parents."

"Do you know where the slave trader lives?" "Of course, I do. He has a grand house not far away. He must have at least four slaves working for him."

"If he's well-off, why does he live in this poor area?" "He'd rather live near people from his own village rather than in a well-to-do neighbourhood where he knows nobody."

We told the minister our story and it was he who suggested we visit the trader. To our immense surprise he said the trader was one of his parishioners. We were too in a hurry to ask him to explain the conundrum. He walked us over and introduced us, without saying who we were, just that we were studying life in the shanty town. The four of us were invited in. "Wouldn't it be fantastic if we get a lead?" whispered Maria.

He had comfortable chairs, a big screen TV and a CD player. Bottles of French spirits stood on the sideboard. No hanging light bulbs here—there were two rather garish plastic chandeliers and wires to a generator outside. The latest model iPhone sat on the table, next to an Apple computer. We had noticed the new Citroen, parked in the driveway.

We told him the story straight. I did half and Maria did half. He listened intently. "These guys shouldn't have taken a young woman with a university education. They never fit in and it leads to trouble." "Have you any idea who kidnapped her?" I asked. "Not really, but I have a thought," he said. "An hour from here, once a month, we traders go to a bar in a lonely, smallish, village in the desert, to swap information and stories and to settle the current prices. I guess we're a kind of cartel. The slaves that are to be newly sold sit under an awning nearby, and sometimes we barter one slave for another. One trader might want a man rather than a woman, or a very strong man instead of a normally built one. We have all morning, so there's no hurry. Some of the guys I know, most I don't. There was one girl who looked educated. The man who had her disappeared. I never saw him again."

Salim took his turn. "When is your next get-together?" "Actually, it's the day after tomorrow. I couldn't take your white friends, but I could probably say you are my assistant."

This was a breakthrough. My heart pounded. Salim fixed a rendezvous for tomorrow; we called a taxi and drove him back to his home. Before long we were sitting down with Ana in the same restaurant as yesterday, sipping cold bottled water, trying to re-hydrate our dried-out bodies. We were almost withering away. She listened intensely to what we had to say. Maria broke into Spanish and the conversation with Ana raced along, seemingly speaking two words for every one word we'd use in English.

"I don't think it wise for you to go tomorrow, I'm glad you have decided that," Ana said. "But what's Salim going to do if he sees this guy—ask him for his phone number and e-mail address?" She smiled. She didn't want us to look like fools. "I think we have to get in touch with the police chief again. I'll phone him right now, if you agree." "Yes, do," we both said.

She punched the buttons, and he answered. We only heard Ana's side of the conversation. She was good at distilling what Maria had said in ten minutes into three or four. Then he was talking — for quite a bit longer.

The conversation ended. Ana said, "That sounded good. His guys had already reported to him for the day and one had picked up about this meeting. He said to tell you, congratulations on your police work! I don't think they have thorough journalists like you in Mauritania. When all this is over I'll arrange for you to come back here to run a course for local journalists."

"He didn't spell it out in detail, but I got the impression that they'll infiltrate the meeting," Ana continued. "But our trader friend who is taking Salim won't want the police there. He will be afraid they will pick him up. He's not going to cooperate."

Maria interrupted. "He doesn't have to know the police are there, but we do have to brief Salim. It will be up to Salim to give some sort of signal to the police agents." Ana called the police chief again. "He asked her to ask us to bring Salim to a bar he named. He would be there in an hour with one of his agents." We had a beer and then I paid up and we hailed a taxi.

Soon we were heading back into the city. Salim knew the bar we were heading for — he seemed to know them all. We had half an hour to wait. We told Salim what was being planned. It took a bit to warm him up. But we stressed that the police chief took this seriously and that he wasn't doing this for a show to impress the American and Spanish diplomats. I slipped Salim €50 and Ana told him if all this led to finding Agnes, her newspaper would give him a substantial payment. He smiled. "Make sure it's enough for a new motorbike!" They high fived and then shook our hands.

The police chief entered, alongside a man who looked the part. Two gold teeth and brand new, pointed, leather shoes, with a crocodile finish. He wanted to talk to Salim. Of course, they talked in Arabic. Salim nodded as he spoke. He was clearly intimidated by the chief of police, a man who until less than an hour ago he never dreamt he would meet. As the conversation proceeded, he seemed to relax. Later he told us the chief had mentioned the government had offered a reward for her safe recovery. Apparently, the Americans had negotiated that.

"It's settled," the police chief said, finishing his orange juice. "We have a plan. I'm not going to give you details, there's no point, but I'm hopeful if will work. I think you three are amazing. We'd picked up about the meeting—or rather the Americans did with their high-powered listening system, far more sophisticated than ours—but we didn't have a way of recognizing your Mr X. But Salim thinks he can talk to one of the traffickers who might know. Great you found him!"

We invited the chief for dinner. He refused, saying it was already late and he wanted to get back to his family. The food looked good so we stayed. Salim ate goat, saying how marvellous it was, especially the innards and eyes. We both settled for couscous and chicken.

Back in the hotel I flopped down on Maria's bed. If all went well tomorrow and we found Agnes this would be my last night in Maria's bed. I felt confused, sad, in turmoil, all mixed up together like a chemical potion whisked into a lather. I'd never in my life had to deal with such contradictory, confusing, emotions. I felt totally out of my depth. This wasn't me, even though, as I thought about the tangle, I could see how I got into it. I thought, well, perhaps this is the real me. I am one of those guys who can't keep his zipper up and I should just come to terms with it and live my life out with a few things kept secret in the cupboard. That didn't sound right. It went against my Christian principles. But how seriously was I attached to those? If I'd grown up in an Islamic society that was just as God-fearing as Christianity and Judaism, I'd be a bit more relaxed and take more than one wife. But I also knew that neither Islam nor Judaism allow pre-marital sex or adultery, although the founder of Judaism and Islam, Abraham, had a wife and mistress at the same time. Jews, Christians and Muslims regard Abraham as the patriarch of their religion, the "father of the faith." King David of Israel had quite a few wives and lovers. His importance to the Jews of today is that he was the founder of Jerusalem. King Solomon, his son, had hundreds of concubines.

My thoughts wandered on rather chaotically, more destructively than constructively. I heard Maria coming out of the bathroom. I sat up. "Come on, we are going to have a swim before bed. And then I am going to sin again. I don't know about you." I guess I looked a bit non-plussed. "If you don't want to I'll phone a male escort service. You've turned me into a randy woman." She giggled and kissed me. Then she tried to look depressed. "I guess they don't have male escort services in this god-forsaken country. It will have to be you." She giggled again. "So let's drink up and you can get yourself into shape for the night with some fast swimming."

We had nothing to do the next day. Things had been taken out of her hands. But then Ana phoned to say she had a day off and would we like to go to the beach. We jumped at the idea. A rather nice old Bentley complete with chauffeur drew up at the hotel.

In an hour we were at a splendid, almost deserted, beach. The sun was still a dim light bulb in the sky. But in the tropics the power of the sun changes fast. By the time we'd changed and chatted a little it was already bright yellow and rising. The sky was serene. Ana warned us that this being the Atlantic the water could be treacherous. The waves often were immensely strong and there were wild currents. Stay close to the shore, she warned. We swam and played around for a good half an hour. Ana then pasted us with sun block, warning that an hour of this sun could give us sunstroke. Thoughtful, she had brought three hats.

"I've brought a picnic lunch," Ana said. It's in the car. Up there are some coconut trees and shade. But coffee first."

The menu was Spanish: fresh sardines in olive oil, Spanish omelette, olives and a fresh loaf. There was cold beer and bubbly Cava in an icebox. "I can't eat local food all the time. I need my Spanish indulgence."

"I wonder how they are getting on?" I mused. "I hope this plan works. Imagine if Agnes were suddenly there, beside us!"

We had one more swim and got into the car and were driven back to the hotel. "Ana, come. Let's see if there's a message with any news."

The three of us walked into the lobby. I couldn't believe it. There was Agnes, along with Salim. She let out an almighty whoop and hurled herself into my arms. I held her tight, finding it impossible not to give her a long kiss, even though Maria was right there.

I introduced her to the others. "These two women are responsible for your release. I put them on my payroll," I said with a wink.

We found a seat outside in the shade. I invited Salim to join us. I studied Agnes. For sure she had lost weight. She was wearing Islamic dress, but of poor quality. She quickly pulled her scarf off. "Life is now precious and sweet. I have it all before me. Tonight, I want to celebrate! It doesn't have to be champagne, just a glass or two or three of wine. Do you realize I've not been allowed alcohol? And no more goat to eat. I want real food—a steak made of beef, French fries and salad. Then for dessert, ice cream and fresh fruit. Do you think they do that here?"

"For sure," I said. "I can see you are badly deprived. We are going to fatten you up and we'll treat you like a princess for a couple of days."

Ana interjected. "We have to have at least one glass of champagne. The prodigal daughter doesn't return every day!"

We were silent while we waited for the drinks to arrive. I think for all of us it was just too much. We had tracked her down—an almost impossible feat. The air had cleared, lifted, lightened. We had got through a very bad time. A huge weight of darkness had been lifted from my mind. Anxiety and fear had transported themselves away, somewhere else. Far away, to the land of the leprechauns of my Irish grandfather, as far as I was concerned.

Agnes couldn't stop smiling at me. She reached out her hand and held mine tight. "If I hadn't had you to think about I'd have gone crazy."

"My melancholy," she continued, "was overwhelming. Sometimes it became apathy but I knew I had to drag myself forward. Why was life intent on whipping me? I kept telling myself that I knew you would search for me."

I could see that Maria was fighting back her tears. I could guess what mixed emotions were going through her mind.

Maria was overcome. She had helped free this woman. She had amazing stories for her newspaper. Tomorrow she would interview Agnes. But she wanted me. Or part of her did. She was committed to her husband and thought she loved him. She had been married in church and had always tried to be a good Catholic, a good person. She had never foreseen a situation like this with me. She wished she'd put the brake on earlier. But then how could she have passed me up, considering her feelings? It was all horrendously difficult. Could she just hand me over to Agnes and get on a plane back home? It really was a bad and utterly confusing situation. Loving can hurt deep into the stomach. She couldn't see a way out. Neither could I. I had the same feelings.

Ana cut into our thoughts. "I'm sure Agnes wants to buy some clothes. Now it's cooled down let's go shopping." "Yes, please. I would be happy to burn this dress," said Agnes.

I'm not crazy about going shopping with females but I certainly did not want to leave these three wonderful women and sit alone with a book. "Ok, let's go! Salim, I don't think this will interest you. Let's meet tomorrow lunch time in that same restaurant and we can sort everything out." Salim nodded and smiled broadly. "I'm very happy for you all," he said. "I've learnt a lot. And earned myself a motorbike!" Ana nodded. "You definitely have. And the Americans are going to give you something too — I suggested to the ambassador they give you a scholarship to study for a degree in America." Salim's face lit up.

We walked off towards the town centre. "What an amazing, first-class guy," I mused aloud, "And so is the police chief. I think we must take his whole family out for dinner this weekend, and Salim's mother. I feel so good. If I had had gold in my pocket I'd go along the street distributing it to anyone who looked poor."

I dreaded the evening. Maria would expect to sleep with me and probably Agnes too. I needed to speak to both women alone and separately.

For now, Maria, Ana and I were fixed on giving Agnes a good time. We shopped and then took her to our beach and, after a long walk, with Agnes paddling and then jumping with joy, ended up in a bar. I ordered four fresh orange juices. Agnes told us her story.

After I'd left to go back to Dakar to fetch our passports she had gone for a walk around the village. Passing the chief's house she knocked on the door. A wife opened the door and invited her in for coffee. Another wife was in the kitchen and the three of them managed to make some sort of conversation in broken French. The chief popped his head around the door and smiled. "Did Jon find a lift?" "He did."

"I stayed an hour or so and then wandered off. I thought I'd go back to the bar where we had met the trafficker. He was there and talking to a couple of hefty looking men. I ordered another coffee and a croissant and started to read the Ben Okri book Jon had left for me. One of the traffickers caught my eye. "Still thinking of crossing the desert?" "I think so. Jon has gone to Dakar to fetch his passport. Then when he gets back at the end of the week perhaps you can give us a lift. Of course, we would pay you." I asked him for his name. It was Ali. "I suppose I could," and he laughed. I could see him wink at his mates. "Let me know when your friend is back—I'm organising a trip but I have to put a full cargo together." "Where do your migrants stay while waiting?" I asked. "Here and there around the town."

"I walked out, set upon continuing my ramble. I cut up an alleyway. I could see a mosque ahead on top of a small hill. I thought it would be cool there and I could meditate a bit. Suddenly I felt the rough hands of a man who pushed me against the wall. Another one handcuffed me. They walked me up towards the mosque and then pushed me into the courtyard of the last house in the street. It was the two men I'd seen with Ali in the café. I screamed, but the streets were dead. Everyone was resting, hiding away from the sun for a couple of hours. One of them pulled out a knife, warning me if I shouted again he'd turn me over and cut my back. I could see what he was thinking. No one needed to explain. I was in effect going to be enslaved. He wasn't going to cut my front as a disfigured me would sell for less.

I was left alone in the little house. As evening approached, I heard the door being unlocked. One of the men was there with a bowl of stew, some bread and a jug of water. As soon as he'd put it on the table he undid my handcuffs. He watched me eat, and then locked me up again and went.

Night fell. There was no light, not even a candle. I couldn't read. I felt desperate. There was no way I could escape through the high window. I was trapped. I was terrified. You have no idea of how deeply I became depressed. Life and its future seemed totally black.

There was a simple bed with no mattress, just string woven across it. Village people had beds like that in Tanzania too and I'd slept on them before — uncomfortable but OK. There was a pail in the corner.

I woke early in the morning sullen and raging. The sun poked through the high window, the shadow of the bars falling on the cement floor. I could hear the roosters calling. It seemed like hours before the same man appeared with a bowl of porridge and a cup of coffee. Again, he freed me. He said nothing while I ate, locked me up again and then left but returned a bit later with a pail of water. "For you to wash," he said curtly. "We leave at 8." "Where are we going?" I could hardly breathe. "Mauritania." He left. I had to wash with my hands locked together.

I was pushed into the back of a big lorry with a dozen girls. I was by far and away the oldest. We had just enough room to sit on the floor. They gave us each a bottle of water and straw hats. One of the men spoke in a loud, commanding voice. "We are going to drive all night and all tomorrow and should arrive in Nouakchott in the evening. There will be two rest stops of one hour, one this evening and one in the morning to eat and go to the toilet."

It was an awful journey. It was so difficult to sleep. We stretched across each other, our legs resting on our neighbour and took it in turns to be the one underneath.

The first stop was dreadful. After we'd eaten the three men singled out three girls. They took them behind the lorry. Judging from the shrieks I assumed they were raping them. At the next morning's stop the same procedure was repeated with new girls. I guess I was 'over the hill' as far as they were concerned. They probably had this male fetish about wanting young virgins.

The desert passed by, desolate, empty, by the hour becoming more alien, arid, and lonely. If music were played it would be atonal. I wondered if any of the girls had been in the desert before. None of the girls close to me spoke English and only spoke a few words of French. These were girls stolen from the bush.

The journey was interminable. When we could see the first houses of the city we all let out a whoop of delight. Perhaps we were already contagious, infused with the Stockholm syndrome. We, sort of willingly, had got somewhat dependent on our captors. Suddenly we turned off and barrelled down a rough track, ending up at a large shack surrounded by a tall fence with barbed wire. We were herded off. Two women were waiting with food and hot water for washing. Clearly, they wanted to keep us looking good since they wanted the highest price possible. There were even mattresses to lie down on.

Over the next two weeks I was a prisoner there. We had three meals a day, a courtyard to walk and play ball in and a plentiful supply of hot water for bathing, heated in two massive pots suspended above a wood fire.

Singly and in twos, day by day, girls were taken off. After a couple of weeks, it was just me left and two other girls. One morning we were told to get in a car. We drove off to some other remote place with a lonely bar on the edge of a village. Other men were arriving. There must have been about twelve of them. Quite a few of them had girls in tow.

Then suddenly there was a fleet of police cars driving up at high speed. They blocked off the parked cars of the traffickers, four policemen ran across the clearing and grabbed us girls. The other policemen rounded up the traffickers and packed them into a van. One guy, not arrested, came up to me and said his name was Salim, that he was helping the police and he would come along in the police car with us and take us to 'your friend' Jon. I nearly swooned. And here I am! I can't believe it. Oh Jesus, thank you, thank you." She hugged each of us in turn, tears pouring into the sand.

Together we told her our side of the story. When we finished I said, "Maria, I can't help but say it—you've got one hell of an article!"

The girls spent a long time telling each other about who they were and what they did. I knew most of it. I dozed on and off and drank a couple of beers. I was mentally exhausted and tired to my boots.

I thought about my predicament. It was clear to me that Maria was the one I was falling in love with, which made it even more complicated than it was already. Agnes, I really liked a lot but the feelings didn't run so deep. Right now, this evening, I had to find a way to make Agnes feel she was very important to me while at the same time I impressed upon Maria that I wanted to bind my life to her, even if the dentist stood in my way. I told myself I'd never do this if children were involved.

In the end it wasn't so difficult. Agnes had been allocated a room on a different floor. Maria and I still had adjoining rooms. Agnes had only made love with me once and it seemed she was mature enough to see I was attached to Maria. I guessed that Agnes, bone tired, would fall asleep as soon as she entered her bedroom and not think too much about me. I whispered to her after dinner that I would be in my room if she needed me but I wasn't going to disturb her as that was the last thing she needed.

In bed with Maria, I told her what I'd said to Agnes. She held on to me tight. "How will I live without you? I'm worried I'm falling in love with you. I'd better get the first plane out." "I'm falling in love too," I confessed. "What do we do?"

She was asleep. I got no reply. When I awoke in the morning she wasn't there, only a note: "My beloved Jon. I had to go to the airport. I found there is an early flight direct to Madrid. I have to see if I can still square life with Alfredo. I owe him a good try. If I can't, I'll write to you. I'll send you a PDF with my articles and you do the same for me. Otherwise, let's keep our wonderful time to ourselves. No phone calls or texts. No e-mails unless I decide I can't live without you. I still think I'm falling in love with you. Maria."

I felt that Muhammad Ali or Joe Louis had hit me hard twice in the stomach. My mind seemed shrunken and utterly dried out with disappointment. I staggered to the bathroom and wretched. Then, my stomach cleared out, feeling better, I thought, quoting Joe Louis, once the heavyweight champion of the world, "Maria, you can run but you can't hide." Maria, I told myself, you won't get away from me so easily. Then I took a shower and dressed and went downstairs. Agnes was already tucked into an English-type breakfast. I told her that Maria had departed in a rush, her story completed she wanted to be in her office to make sure it was properly edited.

"What do we do now? Agnes asked. "Do we continue with this story or have we had enough? I'm game to go on." "I am too. Let's make a plan."

We chewed the cud for a long time. Three coffees later we had reached a consensus. There was no point in travelling with the traffickers and their cargoes anymore — we had seen it all. We would fly to Casablanca and then get the train to the coastal town of Tangier. From there a boat to Gibraltar, a mere one-hour crossing. There were 4 boats a day plus multiple other routes right up to Barcelona in northern Spain. Apparently one can see Spain clearly from the Moroccan coast at the narrow entrance to the Mediterranean. "Good grief, Agnes. I read on Google that there's a flood of people going to and forth to Spain. I'd never realized that Africa and Europe are so closely linked."

We phoned Ana, the Americans, the police chief, his wife and Salim. We invited them all to a celebratory dinner. We told Salim to bring his mother.

"That's a lot of people," worried Agnes. "We can't not do it. They rescued you. Surely, we can charge it to our paper. We can carry it for now."

It turned out to be a feast in the police chief's favourite restaurant. We were given the best table and terrific food. He drank as much wine as we all did and regaled us with tales of criminal activity. We felt we got the inside story of underground life in Nouakchott.

Almost drunk, having said our farewells, we wandered back to the hotel. "Well," said Agnes. "Are we going to sleep together? After all that captivity I'm sex starved." "I don't know," I stuttered.

But the wine had got the better of me and I meekly followed her to her room. I was pretty sure I'd never see Maria again and Agnes and I were going to be travelling together, maybe for a couple of weeks. Making love to pretty Agnes would take my disjointed mind and my hurt stomach off Maria.

Around noon the next day we got the only plane of the day to Casablanca. Then we caught the evening train to Tangier. It was the opposite of Nouakchott. It's a very old city, full of Roman ruins and streets so narrow only the smallest of cars can pass. People were thick on the streets. We decided to stay the night in a small, Arabic-looking, hotel we located. Inside the door it was laid with thick carpets — probably made by child labour. On the walls there were mirrors in gold frames and soft, woven, draperies in between. It had the air of the ages, as if nothing had changed for at least two centuries.

We took a room. As soon as I woke up I realized we better get going. There was no more time for daydreaming. We had to make some decisions, I thought, as Agnes kissed the top of my head and wrapped her arms around me. "You are getting quite good in bed, Jon. For a novice you are surprisingly good!"

"Decisions, Agnes." I raised my voice, a wisp of anger in my tone. Too much was pressing on me all at once. Agnes moved her arms away. "Hey, Jonny boy, take it easy. Let's have breakfast. I need some coffee desperately." "Sorry, Agnes, I didn't mean to sound grumpy. It's just I've been lying here thinking how hard it is doing this research. We've had two calamities. How do we avoid another?"

We ate breakfast quietly. I didn't suggest we have another hour in bed as I would have if she'd been Maria. Instead, I said I thought we should just wander around for a day, breathe in the atmosphere, eat some interesting food and keep an eye out for young black men and women. Perhaps we could get some of them to talk a bit. Then tomorrow we could take a boat across the Med and try and pick up the trail to Paris.

Agnes agreed and we headed for a tourist shop to buy a guidebook to Tangier and a map of Spain. We hit lucky. It had one of Gibraltar too.

"The only three things I know about Tangier," I said as we strolled aimlessly among the old markets in the medina, "is that Tangier used to be the pirate capital of the Med, that in the Second World War and even after it was a great place for spies, and that a famous American novelist lived here for 50 odd years — Paul Bowers. Apparently, he lived in a simple flat and wrote a lot in bed in his single bedroom. His wife, also a good writer, died many years before him. Bertolucci made an exotic film out of one of his first novels, "The Sheltering Sky." It was set around here and in the desert too. I haven't read him for years. Let's see if we can dig out a copy to buy."

That wasn't hard. We soon walked past a bouquiniste — an old grizzled man selling books on the pavement. There it was, the very book the film was based on. On the back it told us that Bowers became a pilgrimage stop for American writers like Tennessee Williams, Truman Capote and Gore Vidal. Vidal described him as one of the twentieth century's greatest writers.

It was getting torridly hot. We found a shaded café and ordered Arabic coffee, half grinds and half liquid. The guidebook told us that the city was a mixture of Berbers, Arabs, Spanish and French. It also quoted Matisse who liked to come to Tangiers to paint, "I've found landscapes here exactly like they are described in Delacroix's paintings," he wrote.

We did the sights—the cathedral, the grand mosque, the ancient library, the port. Agnes wanted to browse the women's shops in the medina. I tagged along, reading Bowles standing up, while she tried on numerous frocks, blouses, sandals……. Then she bought from another shop a couple of sexy bras and knickers and that was that. "Who are they for? Are you in an enticing mood?" "For the moment, it's only you. But the future……?" She gave me a wicked smile. We were ready for lunch.

"Look," Agnes suddenly pointed. "That cheap-looking restaurant. I see some African guys together eating. Let's go there." We sat at the adjoining table and ordered soup, a warm flat bread just out of the café's oven and fresh-squeezed orange juice.

We could hear the Africans talk. Surprisingly they spoke English, although it took me a while to tune in my ear, so accented was their version. Two of them were Nigerian, they told us after we had introduced ourselves. The other four were from Senegal. We told them what we were doing and that we were surprised to know it wasn't just Senegalese and Malians who risked the desert trip. They told us that although Nigeria is much further away they had to try and make it. They were from the Muslim north where a fanatical extremist religious movement, Boko Harem, was shooting up men, women and kidnapping children for no apparent reason. It was impossible to work safely in the fields and food was hard to come by. Nigeria was rich because of its oil, they explained, the economy in the south was full of potential, but up in the north things seemed to be going backwards. Only money sent from relatives in the south gave them a meagre income.

Agnes asked, "So why did you choose to come to Tangier?" The youngest answered: "There are lots of Spanish traffickers who operate out of Tangier. We have found it easy to make contacts. You just go to cafés where you see other Africans. It's all out in the open. No hassles. Tangier is part of Morocco, and the Moroccans don't care as long as we don't try and stay here—and 95% of us don't." "We have come so far so we should keep going," said another, an older Nigerian guy, maybe 30, who we learnt was called Obasanjo and who ended up being our guide. "We want to get to Paris or London where there are plenty of jobs and you are paid three or four times as much as here."

"Can we meet your trafficker?" I asked. "Sure. We are waiting for him. He should be here in the next hour."

"I'm not surprised you choose Tangier. I've read in the papers that Libya is full of migrants who if they are not careful get robbed and beaten up and their money stolen. Some are thrown into rat-infested jails. Some have been made into slaves." They were nodding in agreement. "The country has been chaotic since the British, French and the Americans overthrew Gaddafi. He was a tyrant but not a very bad one as these things go. All the stability has gone."

The Africans nodded again and then Obasanjo added, "I've heard half the boats leaving Libya sink. They pack hundreds of them in rubber boats. There's no problems here in Tangier. We are crossing to Gibraltar tomorrow midnight. No rubber dinghies for us. It will be a small fishing boat. We are paying a bit more but it's worth it. The trafficker told us he chose tomorrow night because there will be no moon."

"Gibraltar? That's where we're going," I interjected. "Do you know where you will stay?" "No, but you can ask the trafficker."

Soon after, a swarthy Moroccan walked in. He smiled at the Africans. His teeth were covered with gold. "Enough gold on that man to sink his boat!" I whispered to Agnes. We left them alone to talk. We could see he had brought six passports—the European, presumably Spanish, ones in a red cover. Tangier's forgers had done their work.

Half an hour later we could see they'd finished their business and we asked if we could talk to him. His English was good. We explained what we were doing. "Could we get a ride on your boat?" I asked. "We'd pay a reasonable price—say double what you charge these guys." He thought for a moment and then said, "Why not? An extra two won't make much difference."

We were all to rendezvous back in this café at 11. "Bring warm clothes," he advised "and some food and water. It only takes an hour but if we hit bad weather I may have to divert the boat. Buy yourselves a strong torch."

"You pay me before we set off. A thousand Euros for the two of you. I'm not going to hold your hand in Gibraltar. I'm going to unload you on an isolated beach and you have to make your own way to town. I'll give you a couple of phone numbers of Spanish guys—the same I've given to these Africans—who can run you up to Paris in the back of their lorries. That's what you have to do if you are going to write an article." He laughed. "I'd make a good journalist, don't you think? I suggest you stay at a little pensione behind King Street. It's called, 'Las Aguas'. A friend of mine owns it."

"As I said before, don't worry about the local police," he said, turning to the Africans. "They know you are only staying a few days and they've got more important things to worry about—like drug and child trafficking. Gibraltar is a den of thieves. God knows why the British want to hang on to it. The Spanish government says it rightly belongs to Spain but I say let the English keep it. It would be a pain in the Spanish arse if Spain took it over."

He gave us a smile with his gold teeth and was out of the door before any of us could say anything more.

At 11 we were back in the café. By midnight, the six Africans and us were sitting on his six metre boat. It had a sizeable cabin with four bunk beds and a small stove for cooking coffee or soup.

It was a calm night. We could easily see the lights of Spain, the sea was placidly calm and an hour or so later he deposited us on a shallow beach. There was a partial moon. It was dark but not too dark—enough light for us to find a path. We clambered up to the top of the cliff. A little while later the path joined a track and we made for the town. An eerie glow from the streetlights lit up the sky. It was all very easy.

"Let's walk with the Africans," whispered Agnes, "and then we can be sure of where they are staying." Twenty minutes later, after they stopped a lone man walking his dog to ask the way, we found the street and then the hostel. We asked them how long they were staying. They shrugged. "Not long," said one. "Once we've found the trafficker, we will be on our way north. There's nothing for us in Spain. The country, we've been told, has no jobs. There's been an economic crisis."

We agreed we would meet them in the morning for breakfast and we walked off to find our own place. In fact, it was just round the corner. The door had been left open for us and within ten minutes we were asleep, dead tired.

We didn't wake until 9 and slightly worried we were late and they had already gone out, so we hurried down to the hostel. They were there, eating a simple breakfast of bread, eggs and coffee. They suggested we join them. One told us they'd already phoned the Spanish trafficker the Moroccan trafficker had given them the number of and been told someone would be around about mid-morning.

They were in good spirits. They had their mobile phones, they'd bought Spanish sim cards from the shop round the corner and had already phoned home to report their safe arrival. Jesus, I thought, this is 21st century migration, not like what I'd grown up knowing about. It was all speeded up, technologically smooth and efficient.

"What are your plans?" I asked. "Where do you want to go?" Four said Paris. "We have people we know there, already working. All of us have got relatives. We know where to go." The two Nigerians said London. Again, they said they had relatives there and it wasn't difficult to find a job. Moreover, the police were less violent.

"How will you get through the tunnel?" I asked. "I've heard the entrance is surrounded by barbed wire, big lights and security guards with dogs. And then when you are caught they send you back home." "I know," the younger of the two replied. "But six months ago, my cousin got through. You just have to be patient and wait for your moment." "But guys have died in the attempt—crushed by a lorry or falling off a train." He looked unfazed. "No pain, no gain." He smiled.

"How do you get the money for this long trip?" I asked. "I can see it's not cheap." "You are right. It's costing each of us around €3,000. I've saved for two years and then my relatives have helped. Once I've got a job I'll have to send them money every month, even after I've paid off my debt to them. But I can earn 12,000 in a year, so it's worth it. I'll only stay three to four years. Then when I've saved up enough money to build a house and pay bride price for a first-class wife I'll go home."

It all sounded so straightforward, but I'd read enough to know it wasn't. If they do return to get married, after a year or two they often have to go back to Europe. The money they've saved goes on the new house and unexpected events. The maize crop has been eaten by locusts or the price of peanuts has gone down or something of the kind. He told me that last year there was a drought, and his village is only slowly recovering. A friend packed up one morning and left for London. Somehow, he made it. His wife thought since he was in London she should be well dressed. Soon enough she was pushing him for money to pay for clothes, then medicines for their sick child and, later, school fees. His wife quickly used up what money he'd earned. He came home for a brief holiday. He had no choice but to make another trip a month later. He hoped in that month at home he'd conceived another baby. So many children died so he needed half a dozen to make sure two or three survived.

At 11:30 a well-dressed Spaniard with spoofy hair turned up. I explained what we were up to. He shrugged and turned to the Africans. He could speak both French and English. He was going to pick them up in a lorry tomorrow morning at 8. The lorry would be carrying citrus fruit. At the back there was a false partition with just enough room for the six of them to lie down. The journey would take around 24 hours with three or four stops to answer the call of nature. There were no customs halts between Spain and France as they were both in the EU. It should be straightforward. They should buy food and water for the journey.

He ignored us, concentrating on the Africans. He wanted payment before they left. The Africans turned their backs on each other and pulled out their euros from their secret hiding places.

"Agnes, I guess we are on our own. What to do?" "Get them to phone us as soon as they reach a French service station and buy French phone cards. Then give us their new numbers." "Brilliant, Agnes, I think you have done this before." I was smitten again. What an endearing, winsome, smile she had!

We went into the bar where they had now moved to. I bought them all a drink and told them our plan. I gave them each €50 and told them if they called us or texted us as soon as they'd bought their French sim cards when we got to Paris I'd give them each another €50.

"Agnes, let's get here by 6:45 in the morning and we can ask the driver at what time he expects to cross the frontier and where he will drop them off in Paris."

We hung around the bar, bought them all another couple of drinks and then told them we were off for a walk to see the town.

"Phew, said Agnes. "I think we are clever. A perfect arrangement. We have nothing to do now but eat and ... Are you tired of my body yet?" "Good God, no. It's too wonderful to be true."

We were up in time to walk round the corner to the hostel at quarter to seven. Soon we were all scoffing breakfast with the Africans. I reminded them how our deal worked. Then they rushed off to the local mini-market and bought their food and water for the journey. I think they were glad of my 50 Euros.

A lorry drew up at the bar. The Africans piled in. There was only a minor risk that the driver would be stopped at the Spanish border. There were too many Spanish commuting to and fro to Gibraltar and the authorities, who anyway didn't see eye-to-eye, felt helpless when faced with the morning rush hour. France and Spain were signed up members of the Schengen agreement that effectively abolished passport controls within most of the EU. So that border was easy too. Only those who were intent on going on to the UK would find it tough. There was no Schengen free passage and there was a tunnel to traverse. It wasn't easy and I'd read that a big shanty town camp had grown up in Calais, close to the mouth of the tunnel, housing mainly the frustrated along with the brave who were prepared to hang on to the underneath of a lorry for an hour while the lorry drove under the sea from France to Britain.

Our plan worked tickety-tickety. Eight hours later we talked to Olusegun, the Nigerian, on the phone. They'd just crossed into France and were lining up for the toilet in a service station. In a few minutes he would have had time to go into the shop and he could give us the number of his new French sim card. That was soon done. We took the precaution of asking him for his friend's number too, Muhammed. We told Obasanjo that in a few days we'd get to Paris and then phone them. All was fixed.

We weren't in a hurry. Let them get to Paris and find somewhere to live. We wandered around the Rock and did the usual things like climbing to the top and looking at the monkey colony. The view of Africa made it look stunningly close. Normally I feel Africa is so far away and Agnes said she'd always felt that about Europe. But here we were but a stone's throw away from each other's continents.

Indeed, because the distance at this point across the Mediterranean was only 45 to 60 minutes on a calm day, in the 15th century Muslims—the so-called Moors of Shakespeare's Othello—had migrated to the mainland in large numbers, named it Andalucía, and built gorgeous, even ethereal, towns like Seville, Granada, Toledo and Cordoba with stunningly constructed mosques, palaces and parks. It became the supreme centre of Islamic learning, producing great architects, philosophers, doctors and mathematicians, much more advanced than was happening in the Middle East or northern Europe. Initially the Muslim forces advanced into France as far north as the Loire. But they were pushed back and, in the end, settled for the southern half of Spain. They integrated with the local Christians and Jews.

It all came undone when in the fifteenth century the Catholic fervents, Ferdinand and Isabella, took over the Spanish throne. Encouraged by the Pope they began the Inquisition in which the Church used torture for the first time in its long history. They forcibly converted the Muslims on pain of torture or even death. Muslim and Jewish businesses were confiscated and by the time in 1492 when Columbus left to discover the New World both Muslims and Jews had gone. They ended up in either present-day Morocco or Constantinople (now Istanbul). They were welcomed—an influx of skilled artisans, professionals and learned men.

"Take me to one of their cities," Agnes ordered as we sat facing the sea in a little café high up, downing a bad Spanish cappuccino—the Spanish found it hard to get it as good as the Italians. I'd told her this potted history and I could tell she really wanted to go.

We agreed we'd look over the town for an hour and then we'd catch the bus to Malaga and from there travel the short distance by train to Granada.

We arrived in Granada mid-evening and found a nice little pensione down an alleyway. The young woman at the desk suggested a couple of restaurants. We were bone hungry and both of us scoffed a large fresh fish, a dorado, and chips. We couldn't wait to get to bed.

It was lunchtime before we became tourists. After breakfast we'd gone back to bed. For some romantic reason—or was it the atmosphere of this almost theatrical city—I felt like a character in a naughty and wild film. We were shivering with love. After, I stood by the window, brazen. I was absolutely and ridiculously high.

We walked over to the small road that took us up to the palace. For Agnes this Arab-flavoured world was all very new. For my part I compared it with gardens, country houses and châteaux I knew in Britain and France. But these gardens were on a different scale. Perched high up on the ridge of the hill, they seemed to go on forever. I had no idea about most of the varieties of flowers, bushes and trees. It was just a mass of summer blooms with reflecting pools and fountains seemingly randomly placed — thrown down from the stars. Each one was tiled differently. The richness of colour and craftsmanship made my eyes limp. An exuberant fecundity. I splashed my face in every fountain we passed.

By the time we got to the buildings we were satiated and gorged with beauty, and the heat was sapping and draining the last of our energy. Granada is said to be the hottest city in Europe.

Again, we were overwhelmed. This time by the delicacy of the stonework, the great golden mirrors, the painted ceilings and highly polished, carved, woodwork. I think we were both a bit taken by the quarters of the Harem. Room after room. "I think a man once in," I said laughing, "would never want to leave this place." "Not so easy," replied Agnes. "Didn't the men have to go out and fight?"

It was balm for the soul. "All we need is an ice cream," suggested Agnes. "That should bring us down to earth." We sat in a small garden with peacocks strutting and swaggering around. I asked her, "If you could live in a Sultan's palace or with me in a pensione making love everyday which would you choose?" "Of course, the sex with you. What would I do in a palace with a harem of 100 girls?" "Ever thought of being a lesbian?!" We laughed at my bad joke.

We had a dreamy life for a couple of weeks. We felt after all that had befallen us we deserved it. We wanted to know more about Andalucía. We travelled by train to nearby Cordoba where the half destroyed grand mosque sat underneath the cathedral, and Seville with the cathedral with an Islamic tower and more beautiful Islamic gardens.

An hour from Seville was the Atlantic Ocean. I consulted my guidebook. Puerto de Santa Maria seemed to be the kind of place we would like — the opposite of Malaga with its tower block hotels. It was a small town, untouched by modern developments.

It was even better than expected. We found a pavement pizza place and sat out enjoying the cool evening air after the heat of Granada. We watched the Spanish perambulating. Everyone looked very smart and elegant. Many women with their dark hair, short dresses and their confident style of walking, looked quite fabulous. We learnt later the town did not attract the masses or many foreigners. It was the well-kept secret of the Madrid and Barcelona upper bourgeoisie and artistic community. We found a small hotel and slept — the peace of the just.

That week we swam on pristine beaches — no plastic bottles or cigarette butts in the sand — and did long walks along the coast. One day we took the ferry across to Cadiz, the old port from which Columbus sailed. Another day we travelled an hour up the coast and just before the Portuguese border found a delightful town, Jerez, in the centre of the sherry region. In one wine cellar we tasted six varieties of sherry.

We didn't have one bad meal. The restaurants were both good and reasonable. The fish absolutely fresh out of the sea that day. We got used to our after-dinner perambulation, part of the Spanish crowd, every so often stopping for a glass of rather good local wine.

There was time to think. Too much time. I thought about the two women in my life. Well, now it was probably only one. Maria had gone home. I was still in a muddle as I weighed the virtues and vices of the two. Frankly, they both had virtues and the vices I could not see. It was a bit like what Churchill said about Russia. "It's a riddle, wrapped in a mystery, inside an enigma."

Three days later, over morning coffee, when we'd had time to wind down, Agnes popped the question, "What do we do next? What's the next chapter in this story?" "Good timing" I replied. "My mind feels refreshed. Let's go through the possibilities. Getting to Paris is the easy part. From Seville there's one of these super 250 kilometre an hour trains to Madrid. You'll be amazed at that. You feel you are flying. From there, there is the French TGV to Paris — same thing. After that we make contact with our African friends and visit them."

"Then what?" Agnes queried. "We see what conditions they live in, what kind of jobs they've got, how the police and the authorities deal with them. Two years ago I was in Paris. You won't believe it but in Paris they wash the sides of the streets every day. Only Africans do it. I supposed they're employed by the municipality. I wonder if they are ever asked for their papers."

Another three days of fun — sea, sex and sand, as they say, and then we were walking to the station. It was a short ride to Seville. Then we were on the fast train to Madrid. Three hours later we were on the whoosh train to Paris, a mere 10 hours, more comfortable than taking a plane, if you added in the stress of two lots of traffic time and airport hassle, including being asked to get to the airport earlier and earlier. It used be half an hour. These days it was two hours. Ridiculous. I told Agnes this. She was curious about all the decisions I made in Europe. She was groping her way around. "I'll tell you a story, Agnes. If you catch a plane in Europe take your own bomb on board with you." She looked at me as if I was nuts. "The chances of there being one bomb on board are say, one in 500,000. But the chance of there being two bombs on the same plane is one in 500 million!"

She laughed, her white teeth radiant against her black skin. How is it that nearly all Africans, whether they live in rain forest or semi-desert, have strong white teeth when most of them have neither toothbrushes nor Colgate?

We got to Paris without a sweat. Trip-Advisor told me about a not-too-expensive pension in the Marais, the old Jewish district where you could still, despite the gentrification and the settlement of the Gentile well-to-do, find Jewish delicatessens, cafes and restaurants.

I called Olusegun. They were ensconced in St Denis in an old, abandoned, factory, close to La Périphérique, the motorway that circles Paris. The construction of it had destroyed or truncated old communities. Its contribution of $CO2$ and noise to the tranquillity of Paris was a big talked-about minus. It had become a sensitive political issue. President Macron had pledged to do something about it. Yesterday's wonder road had become today's monster behemoth.

Obasanjo told us on the phone that he would be back later from the job he'd already found thanks to the African network—he was in an abattoir, doing the not very nice work of slaughtering cattle on a conveyor belt. He said he was surprised how much money he was making and he'd already sent some home.

We arranged to see him and Muhammad later at around six. That suited us. We had time to visit the Louvre—I found the small Leonardo da Vinci paintings that hardly anyone notices as they rush up the long corridor to the Mona Lisa. The woman pointing her finger to the sky always bowls me over. I tried to explain to Agnes why these paintings were so famous, but it was a long way from her experience of art and she found it hard to appreciate a smiling woman with a finger up in the air. I felt like explaining why her arm, finger and figure were so beautifully painted, but then decided not to. One step at a time, I thought. After lunch we went to see the Monet water lilies in an old railway station converted into an art gallery that had used its big curved walls to hang the 20 metre long painting. That Agnes loved. She could see the point of painting flowers and water.

We took the metro to St Paul's, the stop for the Marais, wandered around and found a café that had tea in a pot (unlike most French cafes with their tea bags) and slices of a home-made merengue pie that was so tasty I had a second piece and then felt sick.

"What do you think of Paris?" I asked Agnes. "Every step we take, every place we visit, I'm totally overwhelmed. I've read about Paris and seen it on television but being here is different. Is this real or am I dreaming it?" "Sure, you're dreaming it," I replied.

I decided to use my Google GPS and we worked out a route to the factory. It seemed to be a long way from a metro station. We took a taxi. We crossed La Périphérique and drove on for ten minutes. I had to direct the driver. He told us he didn't mind coming to this neighbourhood in the daytime but he wouldn't if it were dark. "Don't stay around too long as you will never find a taxi. Here's my card with my firm's number."

He dropped us off at the end of a dusty, dirty street with plastic bags skittering and blowing along the gutters. African street cleaners weren't sent here.

The street was nothing but old factories. We could see that a couple were abandoned. Sure enough two Africans strolled out to the street. We asked them if they knew two men called Olusegun and Muhammed from Nigeria and Senegal who had arrived a couple of weeks ago. We were lucky. They did and they pointed to the doorway they had come out of.

We tracked them down easily enough and found nearly the whole gang from Spain crouched down, African village style, around a big pot of home-made brew, drinking. Nobody seemed to be talking. They were clearly exhausted after a long day's work.

A bit back from them were two women cooking dinner, the smoke from the wood, torn down from other parts of the factory, finding its way out through a broken roof.

We went round the group, shaking hands. "Is all well?" I asked. "So, so," one said. "The money is OK but look at this filthy place. We have only four toilets for 40 people and only two taps work. We have to empty buckets of water down the toilet otherwise the muck stays there." I gave them each the €50 I had promised them.

I wanted to ask them if it had been worth the journey but decided not to. I'd not get a balanced answer.

Olusegun and Muhammed arrived. I asked them what they were going to do after dinner. Both said they'd phone home. Olusegun explained they'd found a shop that sold very cheap sim cards — a quarter the price they'd paid in the petrol station when they'd crossed the border.

It was Friday. What were their plans for the weekend? They had to work on Saturday. On Sunday they'd sleep until lunchtime and then go down to the Nord railway station to meet up with compatriots and, if they were lucky, someone they knew from home. Then they'd find a cheap restaurant behind the station where they could get a meal for €8. Muhammed didn't drink but Olusegun would buy a bottle of the cheapest wine — only €3. "It's better than the home-brew the women make."

Agnes asked if we could meet them at the railway station. "We can have a coffee and then we could take you to the cinema if you like. We'll buy the tickets." The men seemed a bit taken aback but nodded.

I wanted to phone a church agency I'd read about in Le Monde which worked with migrants before they closed for the weekend. I stepped outside and quickly had the director on the line. I fibbed a bit and said I was from the International Herald Tribune. He was happy to meet us and suggested a drink at 6 o'clock.

It was still light. I called the taxi firm. Twenty minutes later we crossed the Seine, and the driver quickly found La rue Canard and number 11. A small, bald man was standing at the doorway, accompanied by a youngish, dark haired, woman. We said our "enchantés." The man was the director and the woman was responsible for West African migrants.

We entered the next-door cafe with big mirrors in gold frames hanging behind the bar, against walls papered red. The bar seats were a bright red to match. It's always too noisy on a Friday night, explained the director. Let's sit outside.

Agnes told them our story, but glided over the bio of me, the novice journalist, and said I was a reporter with a top paper, the International Herald Tribune, that printed in over 30 countries and was sold all over the world. They nodded. Like most educated French they knew of the good reputation of the paper, even if they didn't read it.

"The French government is always saying that they're tightening up on immigrant workers," asked Agnes, "but how come they keep arriving? I noticed yesterday wherever we went the street cleaners were all African."

"It's a game," said the French woman—Claudia she was called—speaking workable English. "On one side the government is trying to reassure a population that because of immigration is moving to the right, even though much of their resentment is based on events that are simply fiction. The National Front, the fascist party, get a lot of the votes from rural areas and small towns where they only see blacks and Arabs on television. On the other side you have large employers—like the car manufacturers - pressing the government to allow in more migrants. They are chronically short of labour to do the more menial jobs and night shifts—French workers think they are better than that. Even if a Frenchman is unemployed today he thinks his dignity will be challenged if he takes one of those jobs and his mates back in his neighbourhood bar would mock him. Also, the workers are always fighting against raising the retirement age. Yet they never ask who is going to do their jobs when the birth rate has been so low for so long.

So many immigrants wouldn't be needed if the promise of what they call "globalisation" had been met—retrain the native workers so that they could get better jobs and let the lower paid jobs be replaced by automation and cheaper imports. However, this would cost companies, and governments have been for too long "laissez-faire" — easy going.

"The government has long made a compromise. Working class and farm worker migrants aren't officially allowed in. Of course, if you are a doctor, nurse or computer specialist you are. With them we are robbing Third World countries of their best talent that their home governments have paid to educate and train. In fact, the French government (like other European governments and the US) more or less actively recruits them. As for the unskilled migrants — the New Proletariat, I call them — who come underground, they are allowed to stay with a wink and a nod, but don't get papers or a social security number. If they are unemployed or ill they get nothing, although the hospitals will always admit bad cases. Otherwise, who would do our dirty jobs? Not just cleaning the streets or working with the molten metal in the car factory, they work as chefs in cheap restaurants, in road repair gangs and do the night shifts. In fact, they oil the wheels of much of our economy.

"Because they are off the books they are paid very poorly. When I first came to live in Paris twenty years ago they lived in bidonvilles, shantytowns like in Nairobi or Lagos. Since then, the government has built way out of town and far from work shoddy flats with few shops or amenities, and rehoused them."

"What do the unions say?" I ask. "They are complicit too. They do the double talk, like the government. These are the jobs their members don't want. Nevertheless, it's not as simple as that. The unions don't know quite what to do. Recent academic studies have shown immigrants do hold some working-class wages down. There are some jobs that they do compete with locals to take. But the unions aren't strong enough to make a big fuss over what are only quite small numbers. They would make a fuss and strike if it got worse.

"The government has re-housed many of these immigrants, even though it knows they are illegal. But as fast as they decide to build there comes a new lot. The abandoned buildings get a refill. The government had long been resigned to the traffic as who else would do the dirty jobs. Not the French for sure. The housing estates have gradually become near ghettos. There are few shops. Cinemas and sports grounds are uncommon. Schools are poor, overwhelmed by so many languages and customs. It is the so-called "multiculturalism" in practice. There is little integration. Banlieues, we French call them."

"Oh yes, I've heard about them. Isn't that where half the French football team are recruited?" I interjected. "Sure," said the director. "They've produced more than their fair share of star footballers, not least the 19-year-old prodigy of the French national team, Kylian Mbappé, who was born in Paris of African migrants. At the World Cup in Moscow he became the only teenager ever — apart from Pelé — to score in a final. Scouts from the famous big clubs regularly hang about the local clubs, focussing mainly on the darker skinned boys."

"But they are only a minority. Many children of immigrants seem to be lacking in purpose. They left school with an education that did not qualify them to get decent jobs in French society. They feel the cards are stacked against them. The police are always on their backs. Crime and bad behaviour, practically unknown among their parents, are serious issues."

"Is this African migration different from the Syrian one?" I'd caught a bit of television in our hotel and had seen that the number one item on the news was the mass exodus from bombed-out Syria.

"France," replied the director, "like the rest of Western Europe, is being overwhelmed by a massive tide of immigrants fleeing the murderous wars in Syria and Afghanistan. Chancellor Angela Merkel of Germany decided to take in a million of them. That was an incredibly generous move that caused something of a backlash. Sweden has taken in more per head of its own population than any other country. The east Europeans who had been helped financially beyond measure after they shook off communism refused to extend a helping hand. Bloody selfish bastards. The UK, suffering from being forced into Brexit after a referendum had demanded it, with the antipathy to immigrants being the number one issue that swung the vote, took very few. France took in 20,000 but this was a small number for such a rich, large and prosperous country. We should be ashamed after all Macron's liberal preaching.

"On the other hand, the French are fairly tolerant about illegals coming from their old colonial territories in Africa. It's been going on for so long that the French more or less accept it. Many of the new arrivals live like you found them, in abandoned buildings. Those who have been here longer either find their own lodgings or get tenancies in municipal apartments. The French have always known that these were so-called "target workers." Once they have made what they had hoped for they go back home to their wives and families — usually after a couple of years. Perhaps some will make the journey again and again over their working lives. But most are content with a couple of trips — enough to build a house and buy a motorbike, maybe to start a small shop, car and bike repair shop or some other business. They are a plus for the French — they have no children needing schools. Since they are young they are unlikely to get ill and need hospital treatment."

It was already half past eight and I felt we'd held them up long enough. "Do phone us," said Claudia, "if you want to talk more at the weekend."

My head was spinning. It was a lot to take in. Agnes said the same. We ordered another drink. I saw the café served food. We had no energy to go looking elsewhere and were happy to eat some pot-au-feu — a beef stew. I think, but don't quite remember, we drank a lot, a lot of Calvados. We hailed a taxi and then threw ourselves onto our soft bed with clean sheets. For fifteen seconds I thought of Olusegun and Muhammed on the hard floor. Tomorrow they'd be working to make my life more comfortable. I fell asleep.

For the next few days Agnes and I, pretending we were Jean-Paul Sartre and Simone de Beauvoir, sat in cafes and wrote up what had happened to us so far. Our editor in Johannesburg thought the articles were fantastic and gave us an immense amount of space. They were syndicated all over Africa and we got marvellous comments and praise from our friends in Tanzania.

Agnes and I, the work apparently finished, decided to take another short holiday down on the Loire. The weather was perfect. We hired bikes and visited the magnificent Château d'Amboise. We swam in the river. We stayed in a pretty pension with a welcoming patron. We lolled and rolled in bed. We picnicked by the river eating smelly cheese, crusty bread and a perfumed red wine, straight from one of the local farms. (France's revered former president, Charles de Gaulle, once said, "How can I rule a country with 350 local cheeses?") In the evening we ate in little local bistros. We were, as the saying goes, "not putting off till tomorrow the fun you can have today." It was all too good to be true. It had to end. But *how* were we going to end it?

A phone call interrupted our blissful, elated state. "This is Maria, how are you, Jon? I just wanted to be in touch. After my articles were published things became terrible for me." "Why, what's up, Maria? You don't sound good," I asked. "Alfredo has left me. Can you believe it? He has gone off with a dental hygienist. Well, they will have lots to talk about!" She tried to make a joke between her sobs. "He told me I went away too often."

She started to cry. Agnes was listening so I didn't know quite what to say. "Can I come to visit you at the weekend, and we can talk? Just for a couple of days. I need to get away from Madrid." "Well, yes. Agnes and I have just finished our articles and now we are relaxing a bit in the countryside." (I wanted her to know that Agnes was still in the picture.) "I'll call you when I've booked. Can you get me a room in the same place you are staying?" She rang off.

"Jesus," I said to Agnes. I summarized the conversation. "Why Jesus?" asked Agnes. "I liked her. And she did help us a lot with the articles. If you think I'm jealous I'm not. We are tied together by what we are doing. I don't think what you were up to with Maria can alter that. Besides, I've never told you — I have a boyfriend in Dar-es-Salaam."

So Agnes had her own life. Maria had hers and I suppose I had mine. I felt sick. I realised these women probably thought I was a rather immature young man. I suppose I was.

I knew that when Maria arrived I'd have to choose between Agnes and her. I knew when we were all together in Mauritania I favoured Maria. I suddenly felt emotionally naked. But that was well over a month ago. I'd never expected to see Maria again and had buried myself in Agnes. I began to feel like a real horror. I realised much of my thinking was egotistical drivel. Looking at it from their point of view they'd offered no commitment and for the long run probably only wanted a kind of Platonic friendship. Why was I being so sure that they wanted to get in deep with me? I felt the revelation of my love and tenderness. Did either of them?

Before the unexpected phone call we had already made a plan to return to Paris the next day. On the train Maria called and said she'd be at the hotel by six and we could all have dinner.

That's what happened. To my surprise it was all very relaxed. We drank lots of wine and Maria veered from tears to laughter and back again as she told the story of her husband's sudden departure. Agnes and I wanted to hear all about the dental hygienist. Did she work for Alfredo? Did she have a brain as well as a fast-scraping technique? Was she pretty? What do you think they talk about? Teeth and gums?

Saying goodnight was going to be difficult, I thought. Love can be a demanding and even cruel master. It can be capricious and often eludes diagnose. It was obvious I was sleeping with Maria. But Agnes seemed to take it on the chin and strolled off to her own room. I'd learnt over the years that many if not most urbanised Africans are pretty freewheeling about sex. I wouldn't be surprised if she thought Maria tonight, her tomorrow.

We met for a sober but pleasant breakfast. I told the two women what had been going through my mind.

It would complete the story if I could meet up with one of the Nigerians we met in Gibraltar who seemed determined to give France a miss and look for relatives who had moved to London ten years ago when border controls were not so tight as they are these days. He would probably now be in Calais trying to jump a lorry going down through the Channel tunnel. We could probably get his phone number from Obasanjo.

I said since it would be only a two-day trip to Calais it didn't need all three of us to go since our funds were now running low. "I think Maria should come with me since she speaks good French." I waited for Agnes's reaction. Was she going to blow her top, suspicious I just wanted to be alone with Maria. I reached across the table and took Agnes's hand "No worries. We *are* tied together by a strong rope." What a hypocrite I was—or at least half of one—but I needed to be alone with Maria for 48 hours.

Maria and I left early the following morning. Agnes said she wanted to go and see Versailles. She'd seen a pamphlet about it on the hotel desk. I said I'd call her that evening and tell her what we had discovered.

On the train I decided I didn't want to talk about our relationship. My brain was jumping between euphoria and fear. I wanted to take my mind off the powerful, will-sapping, chemistry that was passing between us. I was determined just to concentrate on what we were supposed to be doing. We shared Le Monde and looked out of the window.

On the way I phoned Obasanjo's Nigerian friend, Joshua. He said he'd come to the station to meet us. He was there waiting, a wide grin on his face, showing two missing front teeth. It was just after midday, so we took him for lunch. He too was pleased to get his €50.

We wanted to know what luck he had had the last month. "This is the first proper meal I've had in weeks," he said, as he wolfed down a thick sausage and frites. "The tunnel is surrounded with a double ring of fences. But I'm not going to give up. Every week a dozen or so clever ones make it."

"The fact is," he continued, "the fencing only runs for about 400 metres in the direction of the town. OK, the road and rail line are patrolled but if it's a cloudy or rainy night they can't see much. The trick is to wait patiently to see if there's a slowdown in the traffic for any reason. It can happen—a lorry driver in front has something wrong with his papers and the police haul him over to question him. It may take them only four to five minutes to get him into the lay-by but that slows the traffic. So the trick is to run like hell and jump on to a lorry whose lock one can break open with only a couple of blows." He pulled out from his rucksack a titanium hammer that can inflict serious damage. "How on earth could you afford that?" "I stole it from a lorry repair garage," he said grinning.

"I've been told the weather tomorrow will be heavy rain. So that should make it easier to avoid the patrols." "What happens if you fail and get arrested?" asked Maria. "They'll put me in some holding centre. Not a prison. The prison is already full. They plan to fly us back home once they've got enough of us from Nigeria to fill a plane. But that will take time. I'm told it's not too difficult to escape from these centres. They're quickly made and have been thrown up overnight."

"So it's worth the risk?" asked Maria. "Yes, it is. Even if tomorrow night 30 or so of us are waiting to jump, three or four will make it. One or two will be arrested at the frontier if the lorry is searched. But they can't search every lorry. It would take hundreds of inspectors and a very long layby, and really slow the traffic. Most of the rest will make a run for it if they see a patrol coming."

"Why have you been here so long and are still here?" I asked. "In the camp we have made a queue. We have a camp committee that makes rules. At last, it's my turn."

"Can we see the camp?" I asked. "Let's go," he said, "We can walk there in 20 minutes."

As we walked Maria quizzed him about the camp and its inmates. "I know you have a brother in London but why do so many want to take such a risk to get to England?" "Many of us have relatives there. You would be surprised how many, especially the guys from Nigeria and Sierra Leone who speak English. Then there are French speakers who have heard that unemployment is lower in Britain. Many say the social security benefits are better but I don't think so from what my brother has told me. But one thing is true: the British police behave much more nicely. They don't knock your door down in the middle of the night."

We reached the camp. It was worse than anything I'd seen in Africa. Talk about lacking the feminine touch. Even the poorest of houses in Africa are swept clean two or three times a day. Here the place was strewn with plastic bags, milk cartons and empty food tins. The "houses" were mainly plastic sheets and the odd tarpaulin. I could see that when it rained it must be dreadful.

"How many do you reckon live here," asked Maria. "I don't know, maybe a hundred and fifty," Joshua replied. "It changes all the time. Every week I get a new neighbour. The old ones either make it or get arrested or go back to Paris or some other big town."

"Where do you go to the toilet?" I asked. "See those blue things over there. The town hall sent those. They do get very dirty and smelly but they do empty them. We have the odd doctor and nurse who come by for a couple of hours every evening — I guess they are the kind ones. There's an old priest and an Imam who drop by."

"What do you do for food?" Maria asked. "I know the answer to that question," I interjected. "Agnes and I visited an organisation helping immigrants. Every three days they run a lorry load of leftovers here, unsold produce, they pick up from the supermarkets in Paris. A new French law makes it a crime for supermarkets to throw away unsold food."

"Maybe, without all this help," I mused aloud, "the camp would be much smaller, just twenty or so men, easier for the police to deal with."

"You could be right in theory," said Maria, "But that's not very Christian, is it?" So Maria is religious, I thought. I liked that even though I was lapsed myself. I couldn't get round the notion that if there is a God he wouldn't need us; it is us that needs him. It's we who have created him. He's a figment of our imagination. Nevertheless, it meant she had principles.

We wandered around. Some men were sleeping, others playing cards, some hanging up their wash—there was a small stream nearby. "What a terrible life," I said to Maria. "All to get a better one. If they stayed home surely it would be better than this. Besides, how do their home villages work without men to do the heavy work, the house repairs and the hoeing for the crops? I'll tell you. The villages just get poorer, so more men want to leave. Of course, once the guys get jobs here in the north money starts to flow home. But meanwhile what is the cost? Women without their menfolk. Kids without fathers. Two lots of old parents with only the wife of one to help look after all of them. Nobody to do the heavy lifting that every farm requires. Men on their own in the north, lonely and prey to prostitutes, drugs and heavy drinking."

"When money starts to arrive in the villages it doesn't go to making the farms more productive. At first, it's just conspicuous consumption: fine dresses for the women, motorbikes for the men when they visit home and financial gifts to the Imam, priest or preacher to build a new mosque or church." "Is it really that bad?" interrupted Maria. "It is. Later, after a few years of this, the more serious and ambitious start to use their money to build themselves a modern house and to invest in a business—anything from motorbike repair to a bakery, a bar or a metal workshop. Then, gradually, the village economy starts to grow but the agriculture which should be its mainstay never recovers."

I was in full flow. All I learnt from Lesotho onwards in my life poured out:

"African governments, too often middle class orientated, careless about the development of poorer agricultural areas, can be quite happy with this. Their migrants are bringing home much-needed foreign exchange. Some of it is spent wisely importing pharmaceuticals or machinery, but too much goes to pay for expensive European or Japanese cars for the nouveau riche or buying rice, imported from Asia, Russia and Ukraine for upmarket consumers, when there are plenty of home-grown carbohydrates which are much more nutritious than white rice, such as cassava, yam and sweet potato."

"Drinks time!" said Maria. Yes, I was going on a bit. We said goodbye to Joshua and his nearby companions and walked back to the town. We ordered a pastis and sat quietly. What was there to say? "Let's go to a film this evening," I suggested. "You won't understand it." "True, but you can whisper in my ear." I leant over and kissed her. The old feelings were coming back at a tremendous speed. The emotional air had turned passionate. The fire of pure being. We never got to the cinema. We checked into a small hotel near the town hall and before a minute had passed we were at it. I felt overwhelmed by waves of happiness. I was drowning in love. Yes, this was real love, many, many degrees more profound than with Agnes. It didn't help the way Maria had dressed. That's not to say that Agnes in her usual jeans and African multi-coloured blouse didn't look good, she did. But there was no competition. Maria had well-cut black slacks. On top, cut low, she wore an emerald green, velvet blouse. It appeared to both lift and round her breasts. With her light olive skin and black, long, straightened hair, she was nothing less than awesome, streamlined perfection.

I'd promised to phone Agnes. Agnes had had a really good time at Versailles and merely wanted to know what time we'd be back tomorrow so she could hear all about it.

We were back in Paris mid-afternoon and rendezvoused with Agnes at the teashop. She was full of Versailles. She's been taken under the wing of a French couple she'd sat next to on the train. They explained they came to Versailles almost once a year and they offered to show her around.

We told her about our visit to Calais. "I think we can tie up the loose ends of our story now" I said. "I think it's becoming much more than an article. We can make a book out of it." Agnes smiled her beautiful smile, her eyes shining. "Where would you get it published?" she asked. "London, I suppose." "In that case let's go to London, all three of us. I want to see how these publishing people work, read some British newspapers and magazines and get myself geared up to do a better job in Tanzania than I have been doing so far. Maybe someone will ask me to write a book on Tanzania, especially if they like ours."

I didn't dare look at Maria. "Well, I suppose, why not? But we must finish the articles first. With three of us at work we should be able to complete them in a couple of days."

Talk about kicking the can down the road. I wanted to escape having to confront both women at the same time. I told the girls that I needed to buy some new socks and underpants. Why didn't they have another cuppa and a girly chat and I'd be back in half an hour. I strode off down to Rue du Faubourg where the big stores were. It took me barely 15 minutes to buy what I needed. I came out of one big shop, turned up a pretty, narrow, side street and plonked myself into the first bar I came to. "Un vase de vin rouge, s'il vous plait, Madame."

I wondered later what the landlady thought of me. I had my forehead resting on fingertips. Every so often I'd have a taste of wine. Then my head would go down and rest on my fingers. I drank another glass. At least an hour had gone by and I still didn't know what to think. I decided after another wine, when at last it did seem to be coming a bit easier, I'd tell Agnes tomorrow, immediately after breakfast. Since we would all be working together the writing might take her mind off the hurt.

That still left the question of sleeping arrangements. I found time to be alone with Maria for a few minutes while Agnes went off to buy sanitary pads. I explained my plan and that she must let me sleep with Agnes one more time. I promised I wouldn't make love. "Don't worry about that," she laughed. "It's all complicated enough without getting all jealous. No doubt when I go back to Madrid it will be difficult to avoid sleeping with Alfredo until we get the house and furniture divided up. Then *you* mustn't be jealous!" She wagged her finger at me, giggling. "Come on, Jon. Grow up. Our double bed is a big one. I couldn't bear to make love to him anymore."

Before we went to bed late that night I phoned Joshua in Calais. We wanted to know if he'd made it to England. A recorded voice answered. But the voice was English. It was his. He'd done it!

We all tumbled up the stairs with me carrying a bottle of Calvados, expensively bought from the bar and three glasses. The next morning I couldn't remember what we'd done or what we'd talked about. As I opened my eyes I realised I was on my own. I was still in my clothes but the girls' clothes were scattered over the chairs. I guess we'd slept three in a bed — well, that was one way of solving the problem. I presumed since I was almost fully dressed nothing untoward had happened. What a pity! I showered, dressed and went downstairs. There they were, eating breakfast.

I knew Agnes had to be told now. "Maria," I said, "You know I have to talk to Agnes. Why don't you wander around this pretty neighbourhood for a while?" To my surprise she looked me straight in the eye and said, "Agnes and I have already talked about it. She's not stupid. She'd picked up the vibe and asked me if it were true that you and I were on the way to becoming a couple." I looked at Agnes. She smiled at me weakly and then began to cry softly. I didn't know what to say. I put my arm around her. Maria took hold of her hand. My eyes watered. I wanted to blow my nose. I pushed my hair back and could feel my hand shaking. My mouth was totally dry. Maria seemed to find the words. "We are two stupid women, both of us falling for this English son-of-a-gun. He should be shot at dawn. But, Agnes, I know love is never easy — as you can see, I'm six years older than you and I've been through turmoil the last couple of years. Even when we are 60 we may not be out of the woods. Love is always lurking in the lay-bys of life, waiting to upend us – it did to my aunt when she was 65. I remember it. She fell in love with one of my late father's friends and walked around for months as if she was a teenager who had just had her first kiss. He was married. He didn't even know my aunt felt like this. In fact, me and my cousin were the only ones that knew! They never got together. Obviously, the love was one-sided.

"Let's all stay close friends. Can we do that, without us getting jealous? Agnes, I really like you very much and I can see why Jon got so drawn to you and you did a lot of difficult stuff together. If we can get this book off the ground in London you and Jon will be writing together over three quarters of it and I'll be contributing less than 25%."

"Girls, I can't think straight anymore. Agnes, thank you for being so sweet and loving and making it a bit easier for me. It wasn't just fun we had together. What happened between us on that journey with all those frightening adventures really brought us close together. I want you always to be my good friend."

Maria turned the conversation. "Should we get on with our articles? Then we have something to show people in London. Let's ask the patron if we can sit here and work." Then she fixed her eyes on me, "Jon, one thing before we get down to work. You have chosen me, you say. But I want you not to live under any illusion. I am not ready for a new relationship of the kind I think you want, and anyway is it practical when we live far apart? You couldn't live in Madrid and work as you don't know Spanish and I don't want to leave the marvellous job I have. I did start to fall in love with you in Africa. But I've been through hell with Alfredo and he's squeezed emotion out of me. If you really love me and want me, you will have to give me a few months until I am able to make a decision."

I was flabbergasted. My world was falling in. Hadn't she just a few minutes ago said something about us becoming a couple? So why now this big caveat? It seemed contradictory. Perhaps she was unsure and was moving forward and backwards like rapid eye movements.

"That's enough talk for now," said Maria. "I'm going to order three glasses of the best wine they have. Then we go to work." She kissed me on the head.

The work was a good idea. I had to concentrate so hard that my romantic troubles were pushed to the back of my mind, at least while I was writing.

It took us two days of slog. Writing, re-writing, reading to each other what we had done, and taking each other's criticism on the chin. It was demanding, exhausting and fun. Maria, the expert journalist of the three of us, made us stop at 5 o'clock. "You get diminishing returns if you go on after. The brain loses its imagination. Tiredness is no recipe for producing good stuff. I suggest we go and see a film or a concert and then have a super meal. We should drink a lot. We all need it. I can't stand romantic dramas. One last thing, Jon, reserve your own bedroom for the next two nights. It will be good for you."

Agnes, I could see, was bemused by the firm, no-nonsense, way Maria handled things. I was literally dumbstruck. I felt my blood cells were totally disturbed and my nerve ends tangled.

We had divided up the work. We all had pieces of the story only we could write. Then there were parts where two of us were together and later three. We would have to feel our way as we went along, explained Maria. "At least the story is chronological," she had said at the onset. "That makes it a good deal easier to write."

The story unfolded. I began to feel excited. So did the others. At 5 we downed tools and went off to find a good old-fashioned bar. We decided on a film. "A Juliette Binoche one", I said. "I long to see her. I've heard so much about her. Isn't she France's best film actress? Let me look in the paper." We found one. A great film. After, following a tip from our hotel manager, we found an excellent steak restaurant, hidden away in an alleyway. It only had six tables. It could have been a romantic spot. Still, it was amazing how much we had to chatter about. I got so buoyed up by the food, wine and conversation that I suddenly said, "I have an idea that will solve everything. Let's make a ménage à trois! It would be extraordinarily sexy and we could have fabulous conversation like this every evening, we would take turns to cook" ... I babbled on and the girls looked cynically amused, eyebrows raised.

The next day we hammered a draft out and we all agreed it was looking pretty good. Maria said her paper had a spot in the Saturday edition that was a full page—about 4,500 words. So that's what we aimed for, but when we made cuts we saved them as we knew we would need them for the book. We sent off the text. One to Madrid, one to Johannesburg with a copy to Dar-es-Salaam.

The next day we took the Eurostar to London, entering the long tunnel at the spot where the Africans were still trying to find a way through. I found myself giving them a little wave. I wondered how many had made it.

The first thing we both wanted to do after my quick, get-to-know-it, three-hour tour of central London, including a coffee stop, was to get through the doors of a bookshop. We were starved for literature, starved of the feel and smell of books.

We had a good lunch and then I said that the time had come to call some literary agents I'd found on Google and get appointments. The three of us divided them up and started dialling.

Agents sometimes take calls without the caller having to fight the secretary. They know that a random call might herald a masterpiece. By the end of the afternoon, we had three agents willing to hear us out the next day.

We didn't get further than the first one. The first agent, Julia, was immediately excited. "I'm sure I can get a publisher interested. It's such a timely story." "What do you think, Fred?" Fred had been looking out of the window. Fred, she told us was her husband, a BBC TV reporter. "I'm just thinking, overhearing you, it would make a great documentary."

"Would you three consider taking a month — we would pay you well — to accompany me and a crew to retrace your steps? We wouldn't do the whole trip, but just the beginning, the middle and the end. What do you say?" I looked at the others. Maria spoke up first. "Can you do a co-production with Spanish TV? I have friends working there." "Sure," said Fred, "I also have some contacts in Madrid and I can probably get the Public Broadcasting System (PBS) in the US on board. The Americans are obsessed with immigration at the moment and they're fascinated by what's going on in Europe. It will help Julia place the book in the US—and in Spain too. So will you guys do it with me?"

We looked at each other. Again, Maria spoke, "I'm for it. It will take my mind off other things." Agnes said, "Yeah." I paused, I took a deep breath, "I'm in too."

"Fred, when will we start?" "I would guess in about two weeks. Give me your phone numbers and emails. Let's meet tomorrow and thrash out the details of the story. Leave the logistics to me and my assistant, Judy."

We shook hands and filed out. "Lunchtime," said Agnes, a big smile on her face, the Tanzanian reporter who a couple of months ago had been working for a small African paper. I walked back in, knocked and put my head around Julia's door. "We want to celebrate. Where is a good lunch place?" "Anywhere in Charlotte Street. It's just four minutes' walk from here."

We walked along Tottenham Court Road. "I bet you and Agnes end up with careers in the BBC," said Maria. "Jon, start some Spanish classes and maybe you get a job as the BBC's Madrid correspondent." That's a Freudian slip, I thought. She *is* thinking about us getting together.

We found a Greek place, ordered a bottle of Retsina, and a large plate of Greek goodies: aubergines, olives, hummus, souvlaki, tzatziki and pitta bread.

We were madly hungry and ordered another bottle. It was fun to be tipsy. "I have a plan," I said. "We meet Fred tomorrow. The next day we split up for a couple of weeks whilst we are waiting for Fred to get organised—he said about two weeks. Maria, I know from what you've been saying you need to get back to Madrid. Agnes, do you have friends in the UK?" "Oh yes, my old Oxford crowd. Most are now in London."

The morning with Fred was good. He'd OK'd it with his chief. To start in two weeks would be about right. His assistant, Judy, was working on a budget. He suggested we film the story backwards. First, the Channel Tunnel, then the Paris factory and workplaces. Perhaps, if he could get it, an interview with President Macron and the President of Senegal. We would ask three or four of the guys for the names and location of their villages and where the traffickers could be found. We'd take introductory letters and presents for their families. "Maybe we will persuade one of them to accompany us. Let me think about that." Then we'd jump to Gibraltar by plane. A boat to Tangier, then Morocco and head for Casablanca by train or plane. Fred said he was longing to stay in that hotel, and that he was going to work a reference to it in the film come hell or high water — "Jon, I'm going to get you to do a face to camera piece in the lobby — I'll make you a star in your first documentary! Maria, you will do quite a few face to camera pieces in Spanish for your edition of the film." Then the next day we'd drive for a few hours towards Mauritania and be back that evening — that would be enough to get the feel for that part of the journey. Then fly to Dakar. He was determined to get interviews with the presidents. "After all," he said, "this is a damn big story with great implications for the future of Africa. They should want to talk to us. Lastly, the train to Bakel, a day there, followed by a day on the trans-Saharan road with the traffickers and their latest cargoes."

We all concurred with the plan. We knew nothing about how television worked and we were in his hands. Fred seemed a nice guy who was confident about what he was doing. Julia had swiftly found a well-known publisher for our book. She was going to negotiate with the BBC on making a common date for book publication and film transmission. We were ecstatic. Fred said he'd keep us up to date by email. How on earth were we going to get time to write the book, we asked Judy. She said we would have to write it on the road. "There's always a lot of hanging around when you are filming. Then there's the editing which we wouldn't be much involved in. Then there is always a wait for a transmission slot. Anyway, we'd done half the work already with our articles."

The three of us went for lunch and then said goodbye to Maria. "See you in two weeks!"

I decided to take Agnes to Cornwall where I used to holiday as a child. Our holiday was gorgeous, even without sex or sleeping together. After the desert and the slums of Paris and Calais, Cornwall seemed like a green, flowered, paradise. We took the coastal path. It meanders for miles and miles, along the coast, close to the waves. It's always up and down, traversing little beaches or bigger harbours, nestling towns with tiny houses, old-fashioned fishing boats and cosy pubs. Pubs, we found, were the best place to find a room — with two single beds. Nearly every evening we ate fish, straight from the sea that day. I felt, as Ben Okri wrote in The Famished Road, "We human beings are small things. Life is great thing." But he also wrote a line which went right to my heart, "It is more difficult to love than to die." I couldn't stop thinking about Maria.

The three of us met up in London, again at the Quaker hotel, as planned. Maria had flown in from Madrid. She'd decided to file for a divorce. She said she felt much calmer having done that. It had been fun in the El País office. Her articles had been well received and now our joint one was about to be run the coming Saturday, and to be continued the following Sunday. The editor had said that while she was in Morocco, he'd allocated her two pages but it was so good that he wanted it to run at even greater length—indeed as we'd written it. Her editor thought her idea of following the BBC film crew would make for an interesting follow-up.

The next day we met up with Fred. Everything was running smoothly, he told us. He had only one serious hitch and that was being allocated a cameraman he wasn't too keen on. In the end after a bit of re-scheduling by his boss he got a talented older man who composed "gorgeous" pictures. He'd travelled everywhere and would be prepared to sleep in the desert if needs be. He had trained with the great cameraman, Walter Lassily, who had filmed the Oscar prize—

winning "Zorba the Greek" and earned himself an Oscar too.

We were to catch a morning train to Calais in two days' time and visit the migrant camp. We'd spend the night there as the main activity was in the evening and night. The next day we'd travel on to Paris and start filming there. Fred would be bringing along his assistant, Judy, so she could deal with bookings for the onward travel. But we'd probably leave her in Casablanca and from there she could fly ahead on to Dakar and follow up on the requests for interviews he had already made. It all sounded tickety-boo. Too easy?

In Calais my remaining contact, Thomas, had disappeared. Hopefully he had also made it to England. We wandered round the camp and the four of us fanned out to talk. Fred told us to find English-speakers who spoke clear English. We had to win their confidence quite quickly so that they'd be prepared to tell us when they were going to try the tunnel. Fred had brought along an old film of his, from the time when he went to South Africa and got an interview with Nelson Mandela. It was a film on African leadership. It also contained an interview with Olusegun Obasanjo who was then the very democratic president of Nigeria. Fred had brought us iPads already loaded to play the films.

After a quick lunch in town we fanned out in the camp. Our preparation and perseverance paid off. The films on our iPads certainly helped. We got some good interviews and met two Nigerians who were going to make an attempt tonight. They showed us the place where they would try and cut through the fence and the type of lorry they'd look for. "Maybe the last shot of the film could be you two guys disappearing into the tunnel, desperately clinging to the roof of a lorry," said Fred. He laughed. So did we and so did they.

The Nigerians liked the idea. We had promised them copies of the final film and iPads and then they could send them back to their families and friends so that they could see what they were up to.

Ten o'clock came round and stealthily we set off for the fence. Cleverly, the men had decided to avoid the camp side of the fence and walked a good kilometre around to the other side. They were right. It was less guarded. "We attack the fence when a train is going by to cover our noise. Of course, we wait for the guards patrolling to have passed our spot." It all had to be synchronised.

We waited close by the fence hidden by trees and bushes. They had bought binoculars and were surveying the land. Suddenly they were off, crouched low. We'd promised to film them only with a long-distance lens. They didn't want us disturbing their operation. The cameraman focussed as tightly as he could as they approached the fence and started to cut it. In two minutes they were through. They waited. Through their binoculars they could see a flat roofed lorry approaching with tarpaulin ropes across, which would enable them to hang on.

In a flash, as the lorry slowed when the driver put his card into the entry machine, they were climbing up the back and on to the roof. The cameraman had run forward alone. He got the shot we had to have.

Back in Calais we celebrated with good food and wine in a bistro on the sea front. Judy was efficient. She'd found us a good restaurant to eat and a nice place to stay. We sat at the table and the cameraman played back what he'd shot. It was good. We were off to a great start.

Both women had made it clear that they wanted their own rooms. I was to be cast into outer sexless darkness.

In Paris Fred got me to interview Muhammed and Olusegun after they had come 'home' from work. The migrants were now working for the municipality, sweeping the streets of Paris—a city that prided itself on its cleanliness, where the cleaning was done every day by men with brooms and water, not machines which can't get into the spaces between parked cars. Then the cameraman and soundman wandered round the factory filming how awful it was.

We three spent time talking to the two men about their village life and who we should ask for when we got there. They gave us lots of contacts, some with phone numbers—the mobile phone revolution has penetrated deep into Africa—In Kenya 90% of the population has them.

Judy had managed to arrange an interview with the head of Paris's street cleaning, Anton. He was Senegalese. He told us he'd been doing this job for over 20 years. He liked France and he liked the new president, Emmanuel Macron, as he was at pains to tell us. "This man is very anti-racist. He's already funded kindergartens for all and he is increasing aid for Africa. He's trying to get all of Europe to help with the refugees. He and Merkel are hard at it."

Fred decided to stop him there and get the rest of what he had to say on camera. It was a fascinating story. Anton himself had arrived illegally. But he'd never had any real problems that he couldn't sort out with the help of an NGO that helped migrants, he explained. He'd also got residence papers when an amnesty for illegal workers was declared. He waxed eloquent about how much more dangerous the desert crossing was in his day when the mobile phone and Google maps weren't available. He got lost three times and only the Bedouins saved him. He told us he was sure that the French government still turned a blind eye to illegal immigrants from West Africa. Compared with the number of Syrians, Afghans, Iraqis, Somalis and Ukrainians they were small beer. It is war-ridden countries that provide the most immigrants. Most of Africa is at peace. For sure, he knew all about the migrants crossing from Libya, drowning or being rescued, 100 people in a cramped inflatable boat sometimes. But this obviously wise man who had seen it all said the present-day rush was because there was a fear the gates to the EU would soon be shut and this was their last chance. The same had happened with the Syrians. Now the mad rush was over. The Syrian migration had fallen almost to nothing. The African migration was down by 75%. He had heard that on the TV news. Africa was poor but it was developing at a steady rate. If a man worked as hard in Africa as he would be made to do in Paris he could find a job at home. Those Europeans who projected increasing numbers of immigrants into the future were extrapolating from a false base.

Fred loved this chat. He said it was just what the film needed. None of us spoke really good French but we got the gist of it. Judy, who had grown up in France, did speak French. She interpreted. She volunteered to get a transcript and translation made straight away.

So far, so good. We flew to Gibraltar the next day. It was a clear blue sky with barely a cloud. The cameraman got some beautiful shots of the Rock and not so distant Morocco. We found the pensione where the Africans had stayed and the restaurant where they had eaten — all good links for the film.

The next day we got a boat to Tangier. We led Fred and the crew to the café where the Africans meet and make contact with a trafficker. As I expected, another group was there. Again, we showed them the film on our iPads. We promised the film would not be transmitted until they were well and truly in France. They all agreed to be interviewed on camera.

They told us they expected the trafficker who would take them to Gibraltar around 11, that evening.

The next job would be to persuade the trafficker to be filmed. Initially he refused. The Africans joined in our conversation. "You could put your back to the camera," one said. Fred said, "That's right. We will only shoot from inside the boat so no one could tell which boat it was."

Fred had a couple of boxes of cigarettes he'd bought on the plane and I had a couple of bottles of good brandy. We put these on the table. Then Fred gave him 1000 Euros for our passage. We put these on the table. He stretched out his hand and Fred shook it.

That night we crossed the Med as we had before, filmed that and the scramble up the darkened beach.

We ended up staying in the same pension round the corner from the migrants' hotel. On the boat Fred encouraged me and Maria to do some interviews. He said that by now we should have got the idea of how to do it.

The next morning we took the regular boat back to Tangier. We caught the train to Casablanca. I introduced the crew to the delights of the Casablanca hotel. We even shot my face-to-camera piece in front of the big photo of Humphrey Bogart. Likewise for Maria. We took a two-day rest, although by the pool Fred, the cameraman, the three women and I spent a good deal of time talking over our next moves.

We needed African migrants to film and talk to, but they were heading in the opposite direction to us. In the end after turning over the problem this way and that we realized we needed the atmosphere of Bakel. There was nothing for it but to fly down to Dakar and start the journey from there, as Agnes and I had done. But before that we'd spend a day on the road going to and from Western Sahara.

Two days later we were in Dakar. Fred and his cameraman got shots of the bustle of the city, both its modern centre and the shanty towns on the outskirts. In the afternoon he filmed an interview with the president. Then we took the night train up to Bakel. Over dinner he told us that the president was quite knowledgeable on the migration subject and told Fred he was committed to pushing Senegal's economy forward so that there would be opportunities for work back home. How many times has that been said, I wondered? The aid agencies and the Western governments behind them hadn't pushed hard enough for fear of being accused of being neo-colonialists. Moreover, relative to the need they were stingy with their money. (Money wasn't really short— look how quickly the North American and European nations found large sums of it to aid Ukraine in its war with Russia).

We'd brought wine, whisky and brandy with us. The crew had bonded well together and everyone seemed to think we were gathering a great story. One by one people returned to their cabins, including Agnes, who left with a wink, leaving only me and Maria. It was the first time we'd been properly alone together for three weeks. We were both a bit tiddled but not tiddled enough to be stupid.

"Now I've had time to think," I said. And then I paused, searching for the right words. "It is you, Maria, I love. It's you I want to spend my life with. It's you I want to work beside, when we can. It's you I want to have a close Spanish family with. It's you I want to eat with, with a long table where all our friends and family sit round, eat good food, drink the best wine — if we are both working, we can afford that" — Maria laughed. I went on, "And have great conversation about all the things that stimulate us — the politics of Spain and Brexit, the art of Spain and Italy, the music of Germany, Austria and Russia. Yes too! I'll show you my beloved Lake District and Scotland. We will go on holiday to St Petersburg, tour the Hermitage and watch the ballet......" I was being carried away. The drink pushed me on. We were still drinking, one glass after another.

Maria gave me a beautiful smile. She took my hand and led me to her cabin.

The early five o'clock dawn woke us up. The scrubland of the savannah rushed by. We could see cows and donkeys and the young girls and boys sent out before breakfast to milk the cows and feed the animals. We were wrapped around each other, bathed in a delicious sweat. We made love again.

When we descended from the train it must have been obvious that something special was going on between me and Maria. I'm sure Agnes noticed it straight away. Actually Agnes, it seemed, judging from her body language, had started a liaison with the cameraman, so that took her mind off us, and was a relief to me. I knew we would remain good friends and that's all that mattered to me.

We had to take the donkey carts into town. Fred had hired a driver in Dakar who was driving a van up with all the equipment. He would probably arrive late tomorrow.

We decided to drive straight to the consul. We knew there were no pensions and perhaps he could help us. He greeted us with open arms. He didn't get many visitors from the civilization of Dakar, much less from Europe. He ordered us cold drinks. Agnes explained what we were trying to do and that we would like to interview him. He beamed. "Of course, I'd be delighted to help you in any way I can, including getting your film shown on Senegalese television. The government will warm to your theme. They don't want to see their most virile young men working elsewhere after the government has spent 20 years on their health and education. Why should the governments of Europe get all that free—young hard-working bodies—off the shelf?"

"Now the Europeans want us to set up so-called reception centres where would-be migrants, instead of risking the dangerous journey could have their case examined by European officials right here. That's a crazy idea if ever there was one. Why would the EU offer any of these guys a residence paper? We don't have a war. There are no refugees. These men are clandestine workers and the only way they can make it is to remain clandestine."

He grabbed the newspaper he'd been reading when we arrived and smacked his thigh with it. "I've never heard such rubbish. I'm so glad," he said, turning to Agnes, "that this film will make the point that development at this end that absorbs labour and raises income is the way to go. The Europeans raped our country, our continent, two hundred years ago. They enslaved many of us. They have a duty to help us now much more than they have so far." I started to clap. The others followed. "Right, time for a beer since we all agree," he said. Fred, who hadn't spoken chimed in, "You'll be great in an interview. I can hear that." The beer arrived. Just in time. I was as parched as the scrubland outside.

He summoned his cook and told him that it was dinner for seven this evening. "I've got plenty of beds. You stay the night here. There's nowhere suitable in the town." We slugged another beer — an early beer but we were feeling rather content with ourselves.

We drove into town. It wasn't even lunchtime yet. Agnes and I said we were going to look up our old friend the chief. I suggested to the others that they go look for some traffickers and check out the town. I don't know if they were amused or not. I didn't look but strode off with Agnes with a smile on my face.

The chief was exceedingly happy to see us. He wanted to hear about our every step. It took at least a couple of hours both to recount it and deal with his questions. Lunch was served by one of wives. Beer was retrieved from a fridge. At the end he said, "I think you two are lucky to be alive. But I did warn you. Never do it again." I told him about the film. "Mon Dieu," he exclaimed. "You really don't understand how lucky you were. By rights, you should have been dead. What do you say in English? A cat has nine lives. You have had eight of them."

We ambled back to the cafés where we had found traffickers before. We bumped into Fred and Maria. They had come up with nothing, although they'd had a good lunch made out of goat's meat with a rich peanut-based sauce.

Obviously, they didn't have Agnes's touch. It helped that Agnes and I were recognised by the café owners. They all wanted to hear our story. Agnes and I were exhausted from telling it. I asked Maria to tell the next person who asked. Although she hadn't experienced the first part of our safari she knew it well enough from living cheek by jowl with us for many weeks.

We settled down for lunch and a chat with anyone who wanted to listen. They were transfixed. They'd never heard the full story of how the traffickers behaved before. "This will be all around the town by this evening," smiled the landlord. "I know it could be risky, but we are going to do it again with the film crew." The landlord looked at us with wide-open eyes. "Isn't once enough?"

By dinner time we had tracked down some traffickers and some migrants who were preparing to go. We made our usual spiel, paid over a chunk of money and promised to meet them at 5.30 at first light in the morning when it was a cool time for driving.

At dawn two open lorries full of men drove northwards into the desert. We followed in our big van, nicely air-conditioned with beer, water and coke buried in ice and a good variety of food. We had tents, sleeping bags, bottled gas stoves and a box full of various medicines the BBC doctor had advised we buy. This was luxury compared with the first time.

It was a fairly uneventful drive to Nouakchott, apart from a couple of flat tires and one man doubling over with stomach pain which seemed to be solved after we had stopped early for the night and he could lie down and swallow some of the many pills we had.

In Nouakchott we looked up friends, Ana in the Spanish embassy, the American ambassador, the police chief and Salim who had helped us. We took the whole gang of our Nouakchott friends out for dinner that night. Naturally they had to hear our story. We asked the others what they had been up to. The Americans said they'd been tracking a mysterious submarine. They thought it was Russian, only to find out after a week that it was South African. "The CIA bosses in Washington were angry that we had misled them. But how can you see the markings half a mile under the sea? Idiots!" said the ambassador so loudly that everyone in the restaurant looked up.

Ana said, "I can't beat that story. But I'll tell you a funny one. As you might know a lot of bull fighting is being closed down in Spain. But we were surprised a couple of weeks ago when we got a call from a man in a hotel here asking if he could come and talk to us about a bullfighting venture he had in mind. He came to see me. He wanted contacts in the government. He thought Mauritania would be the ideal country to build and open a stadium. I've no idea what happened to him. But he had a lean and hungry look. I guess things weren't going well for him in Spain and I presume the other countries he tried. So here he was in Nouakchott of all places."

"Salim, tell us what you have been up to?" "I'm still riding my beautiful 50cc motorbike. All the kids in my neighbourhood think I should be giving them rides 24 hours a day! My big event, as Ana knows, thanks to her and the American ambassador, I got a scholarship to America. I'll spend a term at the University of Columbia doing a basic science course, then next year I'm going to study animal husbandry at Wisconsin university. All thanks to you people," he smiled at Agnes and me.

The next day Fred asked me to interview each of them. All were great talking-heads and Fred seemed content with the way I did it.

We took a couple of days' rest and so did the traffickers. Then we were off north again, heading for Morocco. The first hours were uneventful. Then round a bend we came on a roadblock with tyres burning, giving off a dense black smoke.

We stopped, a good distance away. The traffickers driving in front of us got down from their lorries and went to investigate. Suddenly they ran back, jumped in and raced the trucks round in a semi-circle, throwing up the stones and dust. We followed as they drove away very fast. Five minutes on they slowed down, thinking they were out of harm's way. It was a foolish thing to do. Within minutes, Jeep loads of armed men raced up and surrounded us. They were guerrillas, they said, fighting on behalf of Polisario which had long been fighting to wrest the Western Sahara away from Morocco and make it their own country. They were aided and given refuge by the Marxist regime in neighbouring Algeria and by Gaddafi's successors in adjoining Libya. They said they were confiscating the traffickers' trucks, their cargo and our van. They'd leave us with our film stuff and one bottle of water each and that was that. They'd seen the BBC camera. After grilling Fred and the two traffickers about what we were doing they seemed satisfied and asked him to film them and make sure it got on the TV news.

We hadn't seen a village for the last three hours. We didn't even see a wild animal crossing the road or a bird flying. We were tramping along, rationing our water, lugging our heavy stuff, hoping there would be some passing vehicle. Then we saw a cloud of dust in the distance. Our hopes rose. But as the dust grew nearer we could see it was the guerrillas with the jeeps.

They jumped out, laughing, patting us on our backs. Maybe they'd come to run us to the nearest village or town? Not at all. The leader, a thin, balding, man, explained in French — Judy translated — that when they had got to their camp 20 or so kilometres away they radioed their headquarters to report on our capture and the short film they'd had made. Apparently, their chief on hearing it was a professional BBC team had ordered them to recapture us so that we could make a full-length film. Then, they said, the world could know what Polisario was up to. They made it clear that this was our only choice. We manoeuvred our returned van off the road and headed out into the desert. It was already nightfall when we reached their camp.

Before we left the coast road where we could still get a signal I had googled Polisario to find out more about it. As far as I could see they used to get a lot of attention in the 1980s and 90s but these days they were almost ignored. No wonder they needed us. Fred called his BBC office and was told by his editor to cooperate. Meanwhile, the BBC would be in touch with the Foreign Office, the UK's ministry of foreign affairs. Maybe they could find a way to put diplomatic pressure on Polisario to keep us safe.

We were greeted by a youngish man, a well-built guy, who made us welcome with a good meal and some cold beer. (Believe it or not they had a portable ice-making machine and a small generator!) We asked about the African migrants and were told they'd quickly sold them on to some local traffickers they were in contact with. They'd be driven to Mauritania and sold off as slaves.

We had no choice but to spend part of the afternoon explaining how making a documentary worked and how the BBC would transmit, first to a UK audience and then on BBC World which is seen all over the world, even in China.

Khaled, as he told us he was called, relayed all this to his headquarters by radio. The word came back to drop other activities and to concentrate on facilitating the making of this film.

Needless to say, we filmed their camp and I made my first interview in the Sahara desert.

The next morning we set off early to escape the heat, one behind the other in convoy and then our van at the rear. There wasn't even a track. The sand dunes continued into the far distance, waving in the heat mist.

At eleven when the heat was witheringly unbearable we stopped for lunch and a sleep. A canvas roof was erected above us to give precious shade.

I asked Khaled where was he taking us? Across Algeria, then into Libya and down to the Mediterranean. He reckoned the journey would take less than a week. Once we got into the northern heart of friendly Algeria in a day or two we'd be passing through some small towns where we could refuel with petrol, food and water. Fred shrugged, the cameraman looked at his shoes, the soundman was mute, his face reddened dangerously by the sun. Maria smiled at me. "This is an adventure I never expected us to have. A good test of our love, I think. If we can make it together through all this I guess we'll be prepared for a life together!"

Khaled didn't seem to mind that we slept cuddled up. We used to wait for everyone to fall asleep and then we'd get up and walk away from the camp out of earshot. The moonlight lit our path. Then we'd lie down on the warm sand and make love.

It was a hard grind. Our first stop after thirty-six hours of journey was the armed camp of Polisario's headquarters built around an oasis. As we entered the camp we passed where the soldiers dumped the rubbish, vultures fighting for scraps. We were able to show Khaled's superiors the video of what we'd shot already.

They were clearly impressed and even more so when we interviewed the boss and some of his men, and then played it back for them to look at. There was a small village of Bedouins with their camels next to the camp. They had a couple of village women who cooked and washed for the Polisario men.

By now Fred was getting enthusiastic. "It looks like we will have two great films. After we get to the Med we will have two Med crossings in the can. All the better."

Maria too was in a cheerful mood, often writing in her notebook, preparing a series of articles that she was sure would impress her editor. I was keeping a detailed daily diary. We both thought this would make a useful part of the book.

In our evening chats we learnt a lot about each other — Fred's career, his prize-winning documentaries, his ambitions, his wife and children, later separation and re-marriage. "Jobs like mine, always away from home, take a heavy toll on marriages." He said he'd like to make a feature film rather like Bertolucci's famous film, shot in a remote Moroccan semi-desert village. We told him of the story of how we met but played down our love triangle. One evening, after a particularly good filming day in another village, he turned to me and said "Jon, you are a natural reporter. I'm sure after this the BBC would like to hire you." I told him I'd love to be the BBC's man in Madrid. He smiled, "all things are possible in the BBC." The next day he had another thought. "Maria is a smashing girl. I'd marry her if I were you. Get her pregnant and that will count in your favour when you apply to be a correspondent in Madrid!"

Bit by bit we were building up a history and portrait of Polisario. Talk about Sisyphus trying to push a rock up a big sand dune. They'd been at it for two generations. Sometimes they'd pushed the Moroccan army back. But then Morocco, with US and French help, began to modernise their army's equipment with sophisticated armaments and Polisario was at a serious disadvantage. Gradually, the African countries that had initially supported them peeled away. The UN which used to discuss their plight in the General Assembly had now dropped them from the agenda. Only Algeria and Libya were faithful to their cause. But the Algerian government only allowed them Kalashnikovs, mortars and grenades. Today all they could do were hit-and-run attacks.

We trekked on. Maria and I became closer by the day. Nothing wrong with this union, I thought. Our love had grown from a common purpose in one of the hard tests of life. "This kind of feeling," Thomas Hardy wrote in *Far From the Madding Crowd*, one of my favourites, "is the only love which is stronger than death." I hoped so.

Eventually we crossed the border into Libya. The customs post was a ramshackle affair with soldiers doing no more than smoking cigarettes. It made for some good shots with the armed jeeps crossing the frontier.

We camped that night in a half bombed-out town. Misery. Luckily, we had stocked up on Algerian wine and Khaled found some local women he hired to cook us some fine couscous and vegetables, mixed with small slices of camel meat. Our desert was fresh dates and figs. Not bad, considering the situation!

The next day was a long drive with the checkpoints of various factions slowing us down. We more than matched them gun for gun. They all let us pass.

Libya is a country still at war, not as bad, we were told, in the days that led up to the killing of its long-time president, Muammar Gaddafi, but pretty awful all the same. There is one government in the West, recognised by the UN and another in the East, near the Tunisian border, that controls the shipping-out of Libya's plentiful supplies of oil. Scattered around the country there were other armed factions whose alliances swirled hither and thither, as when the wind blows the desert sands.

Gaddafi had been a mercurial leader to say the least. He lived in a tent with an armed bodyguard of good-looking women. He was a revolutionary socialist, or so he said. With the oil money there should have been enough to make every Libyan well-off. Instead, a good deal of the money trickled away on white elephants and the ostentatious wealth of the upper crust. One of his schemes was to build nuclear weapons. In a feat of diplomacy in 2004 the British Prime Minister, Tony Blair, manage to persuade him to close down the research and ship the enriched uranium out of the country. In return Gaddafi was told Western sanctions would be lifted and that his throne would be left intact.

But in October 2011 Washington, Paris and London betrayed him. Using the excuse of the breakdown of law and order as a grass roots rebellion took hold, they sent in their jets to support the rebels. Gaddafi was tracked down by French military jets, his convoy blown up and Gaddafi himself killed off by the local mob. Since then, Libya has lived in chaos with little chance of stable government in the immediate future. At least Gaddafi had ensured everyone had an income, a house, free medical care, civil peace and education. Today all that is in ruins. President Obama said the Libyan excursion was the worst mistake of his presidency.

Gaddafi had also supported the Polisario, and Polisario still had good contacts with Libyan officials in high positions. We drove down to Tripoli, the capital. Khaled checked us in at what looked like the best hotel in town. I was walking beside him as we entered the hotel. I must have looked surprised as he turned and whispered to me that we could eat and drink what we wanted. Apparently, the foreign ministry always picked up Polisario's bills.

I stepped back a pace and relayed this to Fred. Immediately he asked Khaled to say this on camera and then his cameraman had a bit of fun filming the opulence of the hotel and later Khaled eating a good dinner, having changed into a natty summer suit.

The next day Khaled disappeared for meetings and left to ourselves we went out to the town to capture some vox pop. Our question was how much they knew about Polisario and its campaign. Most didn't but a few did, so then I asked if they thought Libya should go on helping finance it. Some said yes, some said no. Fred picked out the two best and saved them. "There's no point in not doing a rough, preliminary, edit as we go along. It saves the editors in London a lot of time."

I think I was beginning to get the hang of this television thing. I must say it intrigued me and I began to fancy myself as a BBC foreign correspondent.

There wasn't much to do in the boiling hot afternoon so Maria and I lay on the bed and copulated. It seemed to get better and better. After our orgasms we would lie for almost an hour with our lips pressed against the other's, sometimes whispering sweet nothings about our future, sometimes getting serious for a moment and discussing what should we film next to wrap up the Polisario story so we could return to our migrant film. We walked around the hotel garden. The whole world seemed steeped in azure and the fragrance of frangipani. In the end we decided we had no thoughts and we left it to Fred, who was probably at the pool with his crew drinking a cooling beer. We'd planned to rendezvous for drinks at six.

We had a swim before drinks were scheduled. It was super fun after two weeks of sun and sand. Maria's eyes shone every time she looked at me. I suppose mine did too.

After some social chitchat with Fred and the crew over our first drink Fred became serious. "I've been thinking while we're here we should make a film about post-Gaddafi Libya. I've phoned my boss in London but, she said, I think rightly, that we should get the two we are doing on the air first. She said that me and him should do some preliminary research for a film on Libya so that if we came back we could hit the road running." My BBC career was developing. Three films in a row.

We went for dinner in the hotel. We had been advised that it wasn't a good idea to wander around the city at night looking for restaurants. Some nights the city was quiet but quite frequently rebels would pour in and try and seize a neighbourhood.

Fred spoke: "This afternoon I went to the Foreign Ministry and met up with a friend of Polisario. He took me in to meet his pal, a quite senior man. We had a long talk — I won't bother you with all the details — but it came up that tomorrow night a ship would be docking with a clandestine load of automatic weapons for Polisario, sent by Israel. As you all might guess Israel will seize every opportunity to undermine an Arab government and Polisario is a way of regularly giving Morocco a good kick in the butt. We are going to film that ship and the unloading. One more day and evening of filming tomorrow and that's that for this film. The next day or two we'll finish off the migration film."

We did one interview the next morning — with the Foreign Ministry contact. We were down at the docks by 6 in the evening. Our Polisario "friends" were already there. The ship was expected sometime between 8 and 9. They had a large lorry that they'd borrowed from somewhere. "We have to work in the dark," Khaled told me. "We don't want to be hi-jacked by one of these gangs. You know how lawless it is around here. But we know more about fighting than they do, so they'd better not takes us on." Fred, overhearing this, called the crew over and asked Khaled to say that again to camera. He prompted me and then Maria to ask some more questions about where they were going to tonight, where they would drop off the arms and what was their plan after that. It was all riveting stuff.

The ship arrived. The Polisario soldiers and the ship's crew took two hours to unload it. "We are on our way now, to Algiers, where we can store these weapons. You have my phone number. Call as soon as the film is ready, said Khaled." "You know I can send the film to your computer," interjected Fred. "You can? Allah be praised. I can't keep up with you infidels," he said laughing. We all hugged and they drove off into the night.

We met at ten next morning in the hotel's coffee shop. "I don't think we missed a trick with the Polisario film," grinned Fred. "Prize-winning stuff and the immigration film will be even better. So, OK, how do we finish it? I've been Googling since I woke up. Jon, this is the main crossing point of the Med for the Africans, not Tangier. God knows why since they get hell when they pass through Libya and on the other side the Italians, the Greeks and the Maltese hate them. I read that many of the Africans get detained in holding camps here and live in appalling conditions. Some are hired out and are paid so badly they are not much better than slaves. They have no money and can't afford to run away. So we have to film all that first. Then we will do the sea crossing part. Let's discuss that later."

Once again Fred used our Foreign Ministry contact to put us in touch with people in other ministries dealing with the issue, the Ministry of Welfare and the Coastguard.

We got the most awful pictures of Africans in the detention centres. When I interviewed them, I asked why they'd tried to go to Europe via Libya. Hadn't they heard the bad stories before they left home? They had but thought they'd be lucky. The traffickers charged less for this route than the Moroccan one. Also, for many years the Italians and Greeks had been very welcoming. But now all that had changed. They were turning boats back — simple rubber dinghies, but each holding over 50 people — and were giving more speed boats and training to the Libyan coastguard so they could intercept the dinghies before they got very far.

At dinner, Fred told us that tomorrow we should bring our swimsuits or buy them from the hotel shop. He'd dreamt up a plan where I would be in one of the dinghies and the crew would be in a big launch he would hire to film alongside. He was hoping we could go all the way with them to Sicily or Lampedusa, the nearest Italian islands. We'd plaster the boat with "PRESS" signs and hope that we could persuade the Libyan coastguard to let us go out to sea. He was going to load up with Euros to help make that possible.

The next day was spent organising all that — a boat was hired, the signs made, a trafficker contacted (and a lot more Euros spent) and, not least, the weather checked out. It looked like the forecast was good.

It was D-Day. Departure was going to be at dawn. We would pick up our boat in the harbour and rendezvous with the trafficker and the dinghy eight kilometres down the coast in the harbour of a small fishing village. It all went as planned. Fred told me to get into the dinghy and off we went, out to sea. Lampedusa in Italy was only four hours away. I couldn't stand up so I crawled around the dinghy explaining why I was there. Nobody seemed much interested. Mothers clutched their babies and small children sat with a scared frozen look in their eyes. Fathers looked anxiously at the horizon. It was eerie. No one talked. It was funereal in the extreme. I started to get the jitters.

Our big boat was about 10 metres away and I could see the cameraman on the prow filming the dinghy. Behind him stood Agnes and Maria, waiving. Fred had climbed on top of the cabin and it looked like he was shouting instructions to both the cameraman and the ship's captain.

Then they came close. The cameraman and soundman were intent on getting into my boat. Fred had yelled that he wanted some vox pop. The boat edged slowly up to the dinghy, but there was a wind now that we were well out to sea. It was difficult to line up alongside the dinghy. As far as I could see the swell made it impossible. I yelled that to Fred but either he couldn't hear me because of the wind or he didn't want to hear.

It all happened in a second. The cameraman's shoes slipped as he clambered from the boat to the dinghy. His heavy camera fell to the floor. Suddenly we noticed a rip in the rubber and the water started to pour in. Immediately the African men stood up and tried to stretch out to hold on to the bigger boat, but all that happened was that the weight of the first few men pushed away the dinghy from the boat and five of them toppled into the sea. The dinghy had only a few life-vests. The crew of the boat threw life vests to the men in the sea and the rest into the dinghy. It was obvious to everyone there weren't enough to go around. But the more people grabbed the faster the tear in the bottom travelled and the faster the water poured in. Most Africans can't swim and it was clear that most of these couldn't. The women were shrieking hysterically, men were pushing each other violently aside to get close to the side nearest the boat. I panicked. I can swim but the sea was quite rough. I could see Maria distraught, kneeling on the edge of the gunwale, her hands over the side as if she were trying to reach me. I knew I couldn't get past the men crowding on the boat side. I had no choice. I jumped off the other side and started to swim round the back of the dinghy. I kept swallowing water. Waves sloshed over my head. I felt the panic rising inside me. None of the people on the boat could see me. The big engine on the dinghy was still going, unmanned. I was hit right across my body by the propeller.

***

Note: The film was transmitted two months' later. Most of the shot raw material had been safely transmitted to London at every stage of the journey, as Fred wanted to be sure it didn't get lost. The final boat scene was re-created in a large water tank at Pinewood film studios. A look-alike actor stood in for Jon.

It transfixed audiences. It triggered a profound debate on immigration policy all over Western Europe. The President of the European Union Council held a showing of it for present and ex-heads of government at their December meeting. At the film's end the room was totally silent.

Angela Merkel could be seen wiping her eyes. The film was nominated for gold medals at the Cannes, Venice, Bafta and Grammy film awards. It won the Oscar for best documentary.

Fred continued to make successful documentaries. His film on Polisario was well received. Agnes became features editor of her Tanzanian paper and married the love she had before she met Jon. Maria took Jon's place at the medal ceremonies and now has them all lined up next to a photo of Jon in her Madrid apartment. Her articles on her trips with Jon put her on Spain's journalistic map. She became the first female foreign editor of El País. She wrote a successful novel that drew heavily on her romance and trip with Jon, including a vivid telling of the tragedy of Jon's death. She'd divorced the dentist and then stayed single for almost five years. She finally married her boss at the paper, a much older, widowed man, with grown children, who, unlike many younger men, had no problem in accepting a woman more adventurist and a better writer than he was. He was quite content to see Jon's photo and the medals they'd won on the mantel piece in their grand flat just next to the Museo de Reina Sophia.

Nearly all the Africans on the boat drowned. Only eight survived to tell their tale back in the small villages in Senegal where they lived.

***

Afterword

It was wartime. My parents lived in North Mimms, just north of where the London ring road is today. They had fled there after their flat in Baker Street (not the salubrious neighbourhood it is today) had its outer wall torn off by a bomb. My mother, pregnant, was in the bath, possibly exposed to the circling German pilot. My parents retreated to the platform on the tube station where they, like thousands of others, slept in rows deep underground. It was there in the darkness that I had been conceived some months before. Life had to go on.

They went to North Mimms and from there to Chorley, not far from Manchester, an industrial town which housed a factory making ordinance, where my father had been sent, so that we in turn could bomb pregnant German women. Fair is fair in love and war.

The war ended. My father stood with his back to the fire and said it was only "the end of the beginning."

They moved to Oldham when I was four, rather closer than Chorley to Manchester. My father spoke French, which he learnt during what he called his "wild days" in Paris when he was young, so he was able to land a job as export manager of a company manufacturing tea-making urns.

Oldham was a sour, Industrial Revolution-scarred place. The mills with their tall, redbrick, chimneys were everywhere. The town was covered in soot. If you want to see it as it was, Lowry, the great artist, with his matchstick people, captured it well. But poverty meant there was no traffic and we boys, all from the working class apart from me, could play football in the street undisturbed.

The next jump up was a small car and the announcement by my parents that we were moving to suburban Liverpool. I entered the Liverpool Institute High School just a couple of months before I sat the major national exam—the so-called "0" levels. Paul McCartney was my classmate and the class teacher put him in charge of me. We have remained friends.

I met my first girlfriend in church—I was very religious and rejected intercourse, although we did everything else—and we stuck together until my second year at university—in Manchester. At university I met Anne who mildly "seduced" me, even though she knew I had a girlfriend, inviting me to a student dance at Cardiff University where she had been invited to represent the student union. She, an earnest Catholic, after a passionate start, refused me even kissing until we married nearly three years later. (That was to be a source of sexual angst. Once married we had love, we had sex, but we didn't have passion. The three-year freeze had undermined my spontaneity. Seventeen years after we married, I was for the first time unfaithful on a foreign trip. I'd found passion. But I also lost my mind in more ways than one. I still suffer from the memory of our tragic break-up and its consequences for the children. The sex you have read about in the novel is purely my fantasy. The story itself draws on many non-fiction articles I wrote for the London Times, the International Herald Tribune and Encounter magazine.)

That year that I met Anne I had my bachelor's thesis to write. Everyone else in my class was writing on subjects like Lancashire's canal or rail system and how they developed at the time of the Industrial Revolution. The idea of this bored me to death and I was determined to find a way to go to Africa. I had got interested in Africa since reading Father Trevor Huddleston's searing book in the school library, "Naught For Your Comfort." Nelson Mandela said of Huddleston, "No white man has done as much for South Africa as Trevor Huddleston." At university I was active in the Anti-Apartheid movement. I persuaded Oliver Tambo, later to be the president of the African National Congress, to become our president.

I read in The Guardian an article about soil erosion in Basutoland, a British enclave in the mountains of South Africa, which was so impoverished with its eroded soils all its young men had to migrate to Johannesburg to work in the mines, returning to their families only twice a year and living in atrocious barracks in the grounds of the mine.

I went to the library and found a reference book on British colonial territories. I found the name and address of the department of agriculture in Basutoland and wrote a letter to say I wanted to study soil erosion. To my surprise a letter came back offering me a three-month paid internship. The money was enough to pay for my flight and off I went.

They asked me to make a survey of a group of villages up in the mountains. They needed to know how many young men were away and where the differences in exit rates from individual villages correlated with the degree of soil erosion in a village's fields. I lived in a small caravan and travelled round on horseback. There wasn't a road for miles. On one occasion I was invited to lunch by the village chief and offered the eyes of goats cooked in a stew. I delicately ate the sauce and then when he was distracted slipped the eyes into my handkerchief and shoved it into my pocket.

I became obsessed by migration. I learnt the stories of semi-abandoned families, children without fathers except for a month or two a year, women infected by their husbands with syphilis (it was the pre-AIDS era) and the inability of villages to recover from their poverty by implementing the very good anti-erosion ideas of the agricultural department. The men needed to earn now not tomorrow and this work of contouring the hillside and damning the streams needed months of unpaid work.

Emigration, I saw, was a curse. The men during their time at the mine spent a good portion of their wages on booze and prostitutes. The young boys at home grew up without male role models and became lazy at school and obstreperous at home. As I could see it, a broken family wasn't worth its weight in gold. I went back to Manchester, my head revolving around the conflict inherent in migration. From then on immigration became one of the great interests and causes of my life.

With my third-class degree under my belt, I took off to Tanzania and Anne promised to follow me. Tanzania was the destination chosen for me by the United Nations Association, an NGO which sent volunteers to work in poor countries. Tanzania was ruled at that time by the most benign of despots, Julius Nyerere. He was an exceedingly clever man with scintillating, original, ideas on development. In his spare time he translated Shakespeare's Julius Caesar into Swahili. His great idea was to form Ujamaa villages. Instead of a people living straggled all over the countryside they were to be shepherded into small communities where, living cheek by jowl, they would have water and electricity, a clinic and primary school and—here was the catch—farm their land communally. Not likely—no one pooled their father's and grandfather's and great-grandfather's land. Where zealous officials tried to enforce Nyerere's will, even burning down some of the scattered homes, they were met by resistance.

I was "development mad" at the time and wanted to get with the Nyerere program. I was driven up into the Southern Mountains, six hours on a dirt road. It was empty of traffic which was just as well as my driver insisted on driving on the wrong side of the road. At every bend my heart was in my mouth. Today it is a wide tarmac road filled with traffic plus a nearby railway. Tanzania has developed fast.

My driver drove me into the small town of Iringa. The streets were lined with blossoming purple jacaranda trees—a legacy of Germany rule that ended at the end of World War 1 when the British tossed the Germans out and took over the country. They finally left in 1961 and Nyerere took over.

Just at the end of the road was a village that had been incorporated into the growing town. I was to lodge in a village house that the local Catholic priest had once lived in. Compared with the mud-built houses around me it was up-market—built in brick. It had one small bedroom, a simple bathroom and kitchen.

I started work in the Iringa office of the ministry of agriculture. There were two other Europeans, a Tanzanian boss and three Tanzanian assistants. My job, I was told, was to go out into the countryside and give advice to the peasants growing a new crop, tobacco. For the first couple of weeks my boss came with me and showed me what to do and what to tell the farmers. In the evening he'd regularly invite me to dinner in the "posh" neighbourhood, full of bungalows, lush tropical gardens and servants camped in sheds in the corner. I openly made friends with Africans and would often eat with them. Whites in Tanzania were not anti-black like South African whites but they weren't that liberal either. I wasn't their type. Ours was a small office and soon everyone had got to know my opinion on race, colonialism, exploitation and Nyerere's socialism. The character assessment of the young arrival was soon spread around in the Club, a drinking, sports and card-playing place where the Europeans gathered after work and at the weekend. I don't think my boss wanted his colleagues and friends to think I was his friend. From then on I only saw Jim at work. But by then I'd made friends with a couple of Africans and my loneliness was contained.

A year went by. Anne, my girlfriend, taught in a mission school. I worked with the farmers. Migration was becoming a big problem in Tanzania. Farmers were abandoning their fields to their wives and flooding into the town. I recalled my time in Lesotho. (When the British left it changed its name from Basutoland.) I was determined to work to stop migration by helping make the local peasant farming more productive. Fifty years later this still needs to be the priority, not just in Tanzania and southern Africa but in West Africa — the subject of this novel

At night Anne and I would go for a walk under an amazing night sky. It seemed as if every star in the great, unending, universe was there. "Where is God?" I said. "How can one believe when one looks at this sky? Sometimes I find it very hard to believe. Maybe it's because we need a God. But why should God need us? The earth is not even the size of a pin-prick in this vast universe."

"You have to have faith," she replied. "Imagine that your mind is as limited as the pin-prick you talk about. That is why you cannot reach into the mysterious."

"We see all this poverty around us" I went on. "Children dying, old widows labouring in the field, drought last year, men migrating to Dar-es-Salaam, leaving their families behind with all the bad consequences that that entails and no medical help apart from the mission. Is God that brutal? If he wants to create life in this vastness, why on our Earth and why living in that condition? Beyond our galaxy which contains the Milky Way there may be millions of other galaxies and may be other universes. Why should God choose us to be the ones who possess life, with half the world living a life that is often 'poor, nasty, brutish and short', as the philosopher, Thomas Hobbes, said?"

"Where do you think morality comes from?" I said on another of our evening walks. "Even Hitler and Stalin had some form of morality, although mostly they ignored the concept. Look how Hitler loved children and how Stalin encouraged Shostakovich to compose ethereal music, well at least some of the time. Darwin never tried to explain that. He was too intent on studying evolution. The sense of morality being central to our existence can only have come from God. He created us and gave us also a sense of right and wrong. There is such a thing as Natural Law that predates the Jews. Human beings have struggled with this concept for thousands of years—that's why we have the Biblical story of those early human beings, Adam and Eve being tempted by the words of a serpent that enticed Eve to eat the poisonous apple. They knew there was a God. So should we. Monotheistic religion, whether it be Christianity, Islam, or Judaism, binds humanity together. Crimes are still committed, wars happen, some people are paedophiles, migrants are exploited, women and children trafficked, yet most human beings instinctively know these things are wrong. Without that instinctive, natural, morality more crimes would be committed. In fact, there would be anarchy. Why? Because we do have morality. The Neanderthals didn't. But God-made homo-sapiens did. We have built on natural law. That's why although I sometimes have difficulty in believing in God is why I believe in Jesus's teaching. So what is the morality in breaking up families by forcing the men to migrate?" And on I went, seized by the evil of migration.

Anne's teaching continued. She enjoyed it. But I was restless. The world of peasant tobacco farmers in a remote corner of Africa where there was only a dingy library, a cinema that only the urban proletariat seemed to go to, one down-at-heel hotel run by Greeks, and with a seemingly endless wilderness of scrub and

Baobab trees ten minutes' drive away. Adventures of the mind seemed to have stopped here. Anne's house had a wood stove which at this altitude one needed at night. I kept my peace of mind here by reading Alan Bullock's massive tome on Hitler but after a couple of months that was over and I was reduced to reading economic textbooks, World Bank reports and novels — there were a couple with migration as the theme — I'd borrowed from the high school library.

I'd come to Africa to "do good." But I also wanted adventure and some sort of idea where I would go next. I began by trying to start to write for one of Tanzania's national English-language newspapers. I sent them a long article on an idea I had for a United Nations Peace Corps. To my surprise they printed it. I took three days leave from the office and caught the bus for the seven-hour drive to Dar-es-Salaam to meet the editor. He suggested I write a local column. "Thoughts from up-country," they labelled it. Once a month I sent them a piece, perhaps about tobacco farmers, perhaps the local settlement of Greek farmers or the new production by a British settler of fresh milk. I wasn't aware of it but this was the beginning of my fascination with journalism.

I was ambitious. Rather than pottering around the Southern Highlands on my 50cc motorbike to advise small farmers and occasionally to fish for stories, I wanted to go out into the world beyond and find subjects that editors in serious newspapers in the UK and the US would want to print. Or maybe (actually, at that time, preferably) I would like to be an agricultural economist in the ministry of agriculture in Dar-es-Salaam where life was more stimulating than in Iringa.

But whatever I chose, first I had to get my master's degree. I flew to the University of Wisconsin in Madison. Six months' later Anne joined me and 3 days later we were married. Once our degrees were over we moved into the violent all-black ghetto deep in the west side of Chicago and worked on the staff of Martin Luther King, even though we had a new-born baby. One day whilst I was attending a meeting with Dr King a man threatened to shoot his way into our apartment. The neighbours restrained him, persuading him that we were "OK" whites since we worked for Dr King. But Anne, understandably, trapped in the apartment, was badly shaken.

There was to be no going to Africa, Anne said. We had baby Carmen, and Anne insisted that Africa was no place for a baby.

It was difficult to practise agricultural economics in London! Out of financial necessity, I began to write about our experiences with Martin Luther King. They were published. I was interviewed. I was offered an hour to talk about Black Power on the BBC's Third Program (now Radio 3). By default, I became a journalist. I wrote a lot of articles about immigration and Third World development. I didn't really want to become a full-time journalist. I felt it was like looking through a keyhole at real life—that of engineers, doctors, teachers and agricultural economists. But I had no choice.

Fifty plus years later I conceived the subject for this first novel. Migration and its evils on the African continent have remained an enduring interest. Migration became the heart of my novel's story.

***

My conclusion, after a lifetime of studying the migration story, is twofold. The goal must be to limit immigration. It causes too many problems for both migrants and hosts. First, focus attention and resources on developing the villages from whence migrants mostly emigrate. Second, reduce demand for labour in developed countries where people migrate to by raising wages and improving working conditions and retraining in those jobs which immigrants are attracted to. This will have the effect of attracting native workers back into jobs they have deserted. Third, raise the retirement age to 70 so that more jobs are filled by older workers. It means, in short, using home-grown labour better and thus reducing income inequality — which has worsened in all the industrialised countries in recent decades. (Trying to intercept migrants in the Channel Tunnel or in small boats crossing the English Channel or the Mediterranean or building a fence along the Mexican border is next to useless without such policies in place.)

Needless to say, for migrants that are truly refugees from war or natural disaster, (I think of Ukrainians and Syrians rather than the Albanians, the largest group in the boats across the English Channel), the doors of the rich countries must be kept open, but with the understanding that they are only going to be given permission to stay for a limited time and they will be helped to go home once their country or region recovers (with aid from the host).

Home and family are where we all belong.

***

For more about me and what I write about these days, see my website: jonathanpowerjournalist.com

Also see the book I wrote: "Migrant Workers in Western Europe and the United States" in collaboration with Marguerite Garling and Anna Hardman. (Pergamon 1979.) Also see the chapter on migration in my book, "Conundrums of Humanity — The Big Foreign Policy Questions Of Our Day," published by Nijhoff. A later revised and updated version is published by Amazon.

ibidem.eu